JEWELS

IN

TIME

Kathleen Heady

i

Jewels in Time

Author Kathleen Heady

Jewels In Time

Edited by Jake George (www.sagewordsservices.com)

Cover design: Jake George (www.sagewordspublishing.com)

Printed by Sage Words Publishing, (www.sagewordspublishing.com)

ISBN-13: 978-0997096279
ISBN-10: 0997096276

Image credit: Copyright: <a href='https://www.123rf.com/profile_norrie3699'> norrie3699 / 123RF Stock Photo</a>
Lincoln

Jewels in Time

Dedication

For Mack M.

Acknowledgements

Thanks to everyone, whether they realized it or not, who encouraged me to keep going on this new writing adventure. Thanks to my two critique groups, in Pennsylvania and North Carolina, to my friend and fellow writer Liz Rice for reading the manuscript early on, to my family for putting up with this process once again. And thank you, Jake George, for being such an excellent and reliable editor and publisher.

Chapter 1

"The greatest obstacle to being heroic is the doubt whether one may not be going to prove one's self a fool; the truest heroism is to resist the doubt; and the profoundest wisdom, to know when it ought to be resisted, and when obeyed."

Nathaniel Hawthorne

Brianna picked up the stick of charcoal that she had sharpened to a point at one end, and scratched the words of the magic spell on a scrap of birch bark. She lit a new candle and burned the writing, allowing the ashes to fall. Gone but not gone. Using her right hand, she swept the ashes off the table into her left, following the instructions of the spell to the letter. Now she could eat. The ritual had required her to fast for twelve hours, sundown to sun-up. And she had not slept. That was another requirement. To stay awake and open oneself to the night.

A bird chirped once in a nearby tree, and a faint glow appeared in the eastern sky. Dawn was not far away. She had nearly completed the magic spell, the spell her mother had taught her to use to ask for help. Brianna stood and stretched, wrapped her arms around her body and bent from side to side to stretch her stiff muscles. The ritual was over, and the next phase of her life was about to begin. She added kindling to the embers in the hearth and stood watching as the flames caught, blazed up, and steadied. She felt tired but strong. She knew she needed to sleep, but not yet. It was the first time she had completed a spell her mother Marged had taught her, in one of the rare moments when she had provided serious instruction in magic to her daughter. Mostly they had played with magic, and Brianna did some of that herself. When she was too lazy to sweep the floor, for example, she used a simple cleaning spell to do the work. Now her mother was gone, and Brianna needed help, if she was not to suffer the fate of many women suspected of witchcraft.

The young girl wiped the tears off her cheeks, the tears that welled up so often these days. She understood the danger, and why her mother had gone. She was the daughter of a witch, although she had never been accused of witchcraft herself. Still it hurt that Marged had gone without telling her, or even saying goodbye. Once morning when Brianna rose from her bed, she found she was alone.

She dished out a small bowl of porridge from the pot hanging in the hearth. The heat of the embers had kept it warm through the night. She added a little honey for taste and energy and sat at the wooden table, where she had eaten simple meals with her mother for so many years. When she finished, Brianna washed her face in the basin of water she had brought in the night before, brushed her teeth with a twig, and pulled her curly light brown hair back from her face with a leather band. She stepped out the door of the cottage, eager for the gifts of the day, and gazed out at the village where she had been born and spent the thirteen years of her life. Smoke curled from a few chimneys. She walked the length of the village's only street at a deliberate pace, turned around at the far edge of the village and strode back again, slower this time. She saw no one, only a couple of dogs. Something must be wrong. This was the first time she had worked a serious spell on her own, and it was easy to make errors with no one to guide her. Not for the first time, she wished for her mother's help. Brianna was sure she had followed the instructions from her mother's book of spells to the letter. She came out at first light and walked. The first person she saw was supposed to be the one who would help her, but there was no one. Did the spell not work? Had she made a mistake? Should she walk through the village again? As she stood in the dawn light wondering what to do next, a sound made her turn back toward the open door of her cottage. As her eyes adjusted to the dimness of the interior, she saw a woman sitting at her kitchen table. The shape of her face and tilt of her head reminded Brianna of her mother, but the woman's hair was red, streaked with gray. She wore it loose, hanging just below her shoulders, and secured off her forehead with a black velvet band. The simplicity of the band contrasted sharply with the rest of the woman's clothing. She wore a full skirt that reached to the floor. The skirt was of a gauzy material with an elaborate floral design in rose and blue that looked like it was based on a design from the East, such as those brought back by the Crusaders. The fabric sparkled as if studded with gems, blue, red, and blazing white that forced Brianna to shield her eyes from the brightness. The bodice appeared to be soft as lamb's wool, and colored a pale blue gray, or was it green? Brianna blinked and the garment was pink. It was magic, or the early morning light was playing tricks with her eyes. The woman was knitting a bright, bold design that clashed with the vivid colors of her skirt; the finished portion fell down across her lap and brushed the floor. She looked up, and her emerald green eyes met Brianna's blue ones, but she said nothing. Her expression was calm, and a slight smile played around her lips. Her fingers continued to move, forming the stitches from memory, the pattern residing in her fingers more than her mind.

Brianna spoke. "You're not my mother."

The woman's fingers slowed ever so slightly. "No, I'm not. Your mother disappeared as you know. You will never see her again in this world. My name is Andera. I was told you needed help, and so I came." She stopped knitting and set her work on the table. A large orange cat that Brianna had

3

not noticed before raised his head from where he dozed on the other end of the rough wooden table. He gazed at the pile of vibrantly-hued yarn, but seemed to decide that playing with it was not worth the effort, as he lowered his head once more to rest on his paws, large like the rest of him.

"It is not a coincidence that we resemble each other, Brianna. I am your mother's sister." She looked around as if searching for something, and then returned her gaze to her niece, who still stood silhouetted in the doorway. Andera picked up her knitting again. "Come join me. I know you must be exhausted after being up all night. Yes, of course I know that you were up all night creating magic," she added at Brianna's surprised look.

Dropping the shawl that she had worn to ward off the early morning chill, Brianna sat on the chair across from Andera and automatically reached out her hand to stroke the sleeping cat. He raised his head and looked at her before going back to sleep. Andera smiled. "Did your mother tell you she had a sister?"

"Yes, but she didn't like to talk about her family. She said that if she had her way, I would never meet you." Brianna's face reddened as she said the last words. "I'm sorry. I didn't mean to offend you."

"No offense." Andera frowned at her stitches, stopped to count before her fingers began to move again. "Your mother had her reasons for what she did. But I am here now to guide you on the next part of your journey. Let's have a brief talk about your troubles, and then I think you need to sleep. While you are resting, I will prepare something for you to eat later. Do you want something to drink now?" Andera looked around the kitchen, and was satisfied that cooking supplies were ready and available.

"No." Brianna yawned. "You are right. I need to sleep." She looked down at the table, away from the direct gaze of the green eyes that challenged her to speak about why she had summoned help. "I thought it would be someone in the village who would help me," she said at last, still studying the surface of the table, her fingertips tracing the grain of the wood.

"Help rarely comes from where we expect it." Andera held up the length of knitting, nodded as if satisfied with her progress, and continued with the stitches. "You should know that."

The girl smiled. "Yes. I do know that. I've been in this narrow village world too long. That's why I asked for help."

"You want to leave the village?"

"Not necessarily. There are many things about the village that I love." Brianna looked up now, meeting the green eyes fearlessly. "I love the sea. I love the fens. I love the quiet and the calls of the birds. I love the early morning. I love when people treat me with friendship, but that doesn't often happen now." She lowered her eyes and twisted the edge of her sleeve with her fingers.

"Why not?"

"Because the villagers don't trust me." Brianna looked down at the table, and reached out again to the cat who had raised his head to look at her.

Andera watched the girl. "By the way, the cat's name is Orangino. He is your cat."

"My cat?" Brianna withdrew her hand in surprise, but then renewed her rubbing of Orangino's head. He bent his neck in appreciation of her gentle touch.

"Yes. You need him. He will be your friend in your loneliness. And he will be your protection." Andera set her knitting aside, taking care to tuck the loose strands of yarn away out of Orangino's reach. "You say you aren't trusted by the villagers, although you are one of the villagers yourself. You have lived here all your life. But you are right. I sense danger here."

Brianna covered her face with her hands. Her fingers were long and slender and her skin soft, in spite of the cold and the work she performed daily. She was meticulous about massaging lotion into her skin several times a day. Andera touched the younger woman's hand. Her hands, too, were smooth and soft, the skin supple. She resembled Brianna's mother in that sense, too, but Marged rarely sat so still and in such serenity as Andera did. "I need to go soon, Brianna." Her voice was soft, like lamb's wool against her cheek. "But I will return. And you will receive other helpers along the way."

"But what can I do? You said I am in danger." Brianna raised her head. Her eyes brimmed with tears, changing the blue to silver. She was just beginning to trust this woman, and now she said she was leaving.

Andera's gaze swept around the small cottage. She knew it well. Her magical sight had allowed her to watch her niece before her appearance in the cottage that morning. The home that Brianna and her mother Marged had shared consisted of one main room, where the occupants cooked, ate their meals, and did their daily work. One corner held a sleeping mat; that was where Brianna's mother had slept, and Brianna with her until she had grown too big to share a sleeping space with her mother. A ladder led to a small loft room, which had become Brianna's own. She continued to sleep there after her mother disappeared. The girl often sat in her loft to look out over her village. She had no glass in her window, of course. Only the very wealthy could afford glass, but she opened the small window space as often as she could. "Your house is protected. I saw to that before you returned from your walk. As long as you remain in the house nothing can happen."

"But I have to leave sometime. I will need to buy food – and people will think it strange that I don't go out. They already suspect me of being a witch. What will they think when I close myself up in my house?" Her voice had escalated in a shrill crescendo that caused Orangino to curl his front paw over his ear.

"Brianna." Andera spoke barely above a whisper to quiet Brianna's fear. "You have just shown me your weakness. It is not that you have made a mistake in your dealings with the villagers. It is not that you are afraid. Your weakness is that you doubt your own abilities. You must not be afraid to be strong.

"You know as well as I do the source of your strength. You have no more magic within you than anyone else in this village. The difference is that you *believe* in your magic. If you allow yourself to doubt, you will succumb to the danger." Andera touched the tender flesh of Brianna's inner wrist with one slender forefinger, and a tiny eight-pointed star appeared. "This will remind you to remain firm."

Brianna rubbed her forefinger over the small tattoo. The spot stung, just like the tattoo on her shoulder that had been applied with a needle. Her mother had given her that one when she turned thirteen. The small triangle symbolized strength, her mother said, just like her name.

"And remember to rest." Andera was stowing her knitting away in a canvas bag, preparing to leave. "That is one thing that Orangino is very good at teaching. Cats know how to rest. They know how restorative sleep is." The older woman stood, removed a heavy gray cloak from the back of the chair and wrapped it around her shoulders. With her brightly colored, ever-changing costume covered, she looked just like any village woman. "Find value in the quiet times – early in the morning and late at night. Remain in your house for one day. This time tomorrow, you may go out among the villagers and complete your errands. That will allow time for your magic to build. Leave before that time and you put yourself at risk." She caressed Orangino's head and smiled. "Orangino will take care of you. He knows the rules."

Brianna was about to say, *What rules?* when Andera turned and walked briskly out the door. Brianna thought of calling to her, for she left the door wide open, but the woman was walking with long strides to the street and down the road into the village. Three men were walking toward her on their way to the fields, laughing among themselves. They did not so much as glance at Andera. Brianna realized that they couldn't see her. She was cloaked in invisibility.

Chapter 2

"I give you this to take with you: Nothing remains as it was. If you know this, you can begin again, with pure joy in the uprooting."

Judith Minty, *Letters to My Daughters*

Magic Realm - Lincoln Castle

In the magical world that parallels that of mortals, a great meeting was about to take place. Magicians, both male and female, from around the world and from times past and future, arrived at the great castle in Lincoln in what is now known as England. The castle was built at the time of William the Conqueror, a fact which meant little to the magic folk. But a castle is an appropriate spot for a meeting outside the realm of mortal human beings. There were many corridors, staircases, turrets and battlements with hiding places for mortal and magical beings. Lincoln Castle was only a little more than a hundred years old at the time we are speaking of, but it already had its share of bloodshed and mysterious occurrences. There were parts of the castle where the inhabitants feared to venture alone. A wispy long skirt had been sighted just out of the corner of an eye, and then it disappeared through a wall where there was no door. Food disappeared from the kitchen where it was being saved for the next meal, and no amount of scolding or even a beating administered by the cook could identify a culprit. Sometimes an apple or a slice of bread was found where none had been before, or food appeared that was unrecognizable to dwellers of a particular century. The soft, pale sticks in a packet labeled "French fries?" What was that?

The magical population encouraged the belief in spirits because it afforded protection for them. In fact, there were no ghosts. What the mortal residents of the castle believed to be ghosts were actually magical people traveling from one time period to another. Now with everyone arriving for this great conference, there would be increased activity. Magical folks would be arriving through the many portals that were found scattered conveniently around the countryside and in the cities. The English people were in turmoil as it was -- not an unusual occurrence in the year 1216 -- and the magical people had a duty to perform. They believed in their ancient obligation to guide mortals to become better people, but with a minimum of outright interference in the events of the world.

*****

Andera strode into the great room where her father Jonathan stood warming his hands at the fire. Jonathan had been old as long as Andera could remember, from when she was a tiny girl sitting on his knee. He had lived for centuries, she guessed, or maybe he had never inhabited a young body at all. But despite his gnarled hands, lined face, and long white hair, he exhibited a strength like no man she had ever met. He turned when his daughter entered the room. A broad smile crinkled his face as he held out his hands to her. "Andera! How did it go with your niece?"

Andera allowed her hands to be swallowed up in his. She was a tall woman with strength of mind and body, just like his, but she always felt like a little girl again in his presence. She let him take her hands and stood on tiptoe to kiss his cheek. He might be the most powerful wizard in the British Isles, and one of the most powerful in the world, but he was still her papa. She stepped back and smiled at him, dimples crinkling her face. "It went well. I left Orangino there to look out for her, but she has strong magic, Father. I could feel it. Marged taught her a smattering of spells and potions, but I think just for fun, to entertain her. And Brianna may not know it, but I think she senses the bigger picture. She knows the magic world is bigger than her cottage and village, and the orange cat is not just to keep her company."

"That orange cat." Jonathan smiled ruefully. "That cat has been looking out for young witches and wizards for centuries. If he can't keep her safe, no one can."

"Do you think she is in danger?" Andera looked into her father's eyes, a deep turquoise blue that could hypnotize.

"Someone with magical powers living in the mortal world is always in danger, but maybe no more than the mortals themselves. Brianna needs to learn who she is, and her place in both worlds. Until she does this, she may be in more danger than most of us. With such strong magic from both sides of her family, there could be problems until she learns how to use it." The great wizard stretched out his arm, and a large raven left its perch and landed soundlessly on his shoulder. "What do you think, Mandor? Was my blessing at her birth, the pressure of my thumb between her brows, enough to keep her safe?" The great bird rubbed his beak against his master's cheek.

A soft breeze caused the flames to flicker as the door opened and Andera's mother Rhys slipped into the room. "Andera! So happy to see that you have returned. I trust all went well with Brianna?" The woman studied her daughter's face for a moment. "Good." She nodded. "Jonathan dear. The folk have gathered in the great hall and are waiting for you." She crossed the room and placed her hand on her husband's cheek. "Come. Everyone wants to hear what you have to say."

The three of them left the room and descended a staircase to the next lower level of the castle. Andera stepped forward toward a small door that had been built for storage of weapons. She bent her head and pushed against the door which didn't move, but she slipped easily through to the great hall where a few hundred witches and wizards were gathered from around the island. They had moved forward in time to the nineteenth century so they could have their gathering in peace. By that time the castle was no longer inhabited, and a few ghostly glimmers would only serve to keep the townspeople away.

The assembly quieted as Jonathan stepped to the raised platform at the front of the room. Andera and her mother slipped in among the folks in the first row, who courteously moved aside to make room for them. Jonathan raised his hands and let his gaze travel around the room, where the light of some twenty torches cast flickering light over their faces. "Thank you all for coming here so promptly. As you know, the purpose of our existence here in this world that parallels the world of mortals is to assist them when they are on the verge of committing a grave error." He paused to sip something from a silver goblet handed to him by a serving girl dressed in a shimmering silver dress that brushed the floor. He handed it back to her with a nod and a smile and looked out over his audience. "You have seen the turmoil in England in the time of King John. You are aware of his selfishness, the greed of his nobles. Although they make much of their Magna Carta, it is a document for the rich. The plight of the peasants will change not at all."

Many in the crowd nodded. Most of them lived as peasants when they resided in the mortal world, and they knew the oppression and grinding poverty that those people felt. Before they could begin to talk among themselves, Jonathan cleared his throat to bring their attention back to him and continued speaking. "King John brings his treasure, the jewels and other valuables that represent his kingship in the country of England, wherever he goes. Because he wants it close to him, or is afraid it will be stolen, or both, it is difficult to say." Again the great wizard gazed out over the folk who had gathered. "We will take his treasure from him, but not for ourselves. We have no need of such things. But to teach the King, his nobles, and yes, all the people of England for generations, a lesson. The treasures of England will disappear into the magical realm, and only be returned when the people have learned that jewels will not make them happy. And that may be never."

People were murmuring now. They could see the merit in what Jonathan planned to do. But where? How? This deed would have to be done in such a way that no mortals could be blamed, for that would simply set them against each other. Jonathan spoke again. "King John is progressing north to Swineshead Abbey. The Wash is an unpredictable kind of place, with tides that can sweep in from the sea unexpectedly for the unwary." He called out the names of three witches and two wizards to join him, all strong, serious workers of magic. "The rest of you may return to the time and place where you are living your magical life. We have some refreshment for you to enjoy before you go, and once again I thank you for coming to hear this news."

Rhys and Andera stood, and as they did so a long table laden with small sandwiches and bowls of fruit appeared at the back of the room. When it had settled into place, another table seemed to emerge from the floor, this one covered in plates of sweets of all kinds, from honey cakes of the medieval time period to chocolate chip cookies, a gift from the twentieth century.

Chapter 3

"Our doubts are traitors,
and make us lose the good we oft might win,
by fearing to attempt."

William Shakespeare

Questions crowded Brianna's mind. What was she supposed to do for twenty-four hours while she allowed her magic to build? And what if someone came to the door? Would she be safe? Andera had instructed her to remain inside the cottage, so she would be safe indoors. Orangino would take care of her. But how was a cat going to take care of her? He was curled up sleeping on the table.

The star tattoo on her wrist began to tingle. She glanced down and started to scratch it, when she noticed that one point of the star, the point aiming toward her hand, had turned a fiery red. "This will remind you to stay firm." She remembered Andera's words. It seemed it had just reminded her to believe in her magic.

The villagers believed that her mother was dead, but Brianna wasn't so sure. Andera told her niece that she would not see her mother in this life, but that didn't mean that she was dead. She remembered everything her mother taught her about magic before she went away, although she knew there was much more to learn. She had enough knowledge to create the potion using herbs they gathered in the forest, and she worked the spell that brought Andera to her this morning. But had her mother taught her that spell, or had she only read it in the spell book she left behind? Brianna had no idea. Her mother rarely taught her useful spells, and never talked about a future when Brianna would need to be on her own. With her mother, it had always been about the moment, and there was joy and fun in the moment, and that was enough.

The redness on her arm subsided. Maybe it was just a test to see if she would pay attention. Brianna stood and stretched. The sun was high in the sky.

Orangino opened one eye to look at her, then closed it and went back to sleep. "I'll get busy and clean the cottage," Brianna said to the cat. "It will help the time pass."

She started with the kitchen, washing the few dishes and scrubbing the worn table top. The repetitive motions of her hands performing the household tasks made her think of her mother. They had spoken of so many things, but why had her mother never told her about her sister Andera? Brianna swept the floor and pushed the dust out the door, careful not to step even so far as the threshold. She brushed the leather flap that served as a window covering and wiped the sides of the ladder leading up to her sleeping loft. She wanted to air her bedding, but that chore would have to wait until she could go outdoors. Brianna became so involved in her cleaning that she unthinkingly put one foot across the threshold as she cleaned the door. She stopped when Orangino stretched and emitted a "Meow." He sat up and looked at her in his inscrutable cat manner.

"Oh, right. I can't go outside, can I? Thanks for reminding me." She set down her bucket and walked over to where Orangino sat, alert now. He fixed his green-eyed gaze on her and Brianna was drawn to sit down and rub her hand along his luxurious orange coat. "So that's how you do it," she whispered, and he answered her with a butt of his head on her chin.

"Witch!" The sound of a boy's voice was followed by a thump – no, a splat. Brianna jumped and narrowly missed kicking over her bucket of water. Orangino turned his green-eyed stare to the source of the sound but continued to sit in serenity. A nasty smell of human or animal waste, the dirty washing water, but their unwelcome gift would have to stay in its place for now. What other attacks would happen before tomorrow morning, when her magic was strong enough for her to go out into the village? And did the people of the village really believe she was a witch? Her mother had cautioned her never to use that word. "You and I are not witches," she had told her daughter. "We are ordinary females with magical powers." Then what did it mean to be a witch? Wasn't that what a witch was?

Brianna moved the pail of water to the corner of the kitchen so she would not knock it over. She didn't even dare open the door now to dump out the dirty water. It would have to wait until later. Tired of cleaning, she took a small jug of fresh water to her sleeping loft. She would wash as best she could and put on clean clothing. At least she could feel comfortable. She liked the idea of being able to look out from the height of the loft., and she would have a better view if anyone else approached the house. Orangino followed her up to the loft, as she knew he would. He leapt gracefully up the ladder steps before settling into a comfortable spot on the floor where he could keep an eye on Brianna.

She found a clean washing cloth and a bar of the mild soap she made herself and bathed as well as she could. She stood in her shift, not wanting to be totally naked when there could be someone watching the house. Her thoughts drifted back to the days when she and her mother would go to the spring outside the village and bath in the moonlight in the summer months. The water there was warm and smelled of the earth, while the moon provided just enough light that they could see to bathe and relax. It had been a wonderful, special mother and daughter time, until the night they were caught by villagers who heard their quiet voices and came to investigate. No matter that they were minding their own business in the middle of the night. That was when the talk of witches began, and the moonlight bathing ended. From then on Brianna and her mother carried water to the house for their baths.

Dressed again, Brianna brushed her soft brown hair and tied it back from her face. The afternoon stretched ahead of her. She couldn't go out, and the house was clean. She could cook. She could read her mother's books, lying hidden beneath the sleeping mat downstairs after the talk of witches began. But now that she was confined until tomorrow morning, all she wanted to do was go out. She paced from wall to wall in her loft room. In the distance she could see a few of the villagers going about their business, but they were not headed in this direction, nor did the group she saw congregated at the end of the street seem to be paying any attention to her cottage. Suddenly tired after being up all night, she sat down on her bed. Surely Orangino would let her know if any danger approached, and sleep would be welcome and refreshing. Brianna stretched out on the bed and closed her eyes.

Her mother was standing before her, dressed in the same blue dress and brown apron that she was wearing the day she disappeared, and she carried the same basket of herbs, covered with a cloth, that she used every time she went out to gather supplies.

"Mama?" Brianna reached out her hand, or thought she did in her dreamlike state.

"Not yet, Brianna. Andera and Orangino will show you what to do now. I thought I could keep you from them, but it seems I cannot." The woman chuckled softly. "You will be fine, and I still have some tricks up my sleeve."

Brianna sank into a deep sleep, and awoke with the memory of her mother's visit – she did not believe it was a dream – fresh in her mind. So her mother knew about Andera and Orangino. Did that mean her mother was dead or in the magical world? She just didn't know. Her education as a magical woman was so lacking. Brianna opened her eyes and saw the orange cat, sitting with his paws tucked under his body, keeping watch. She remembered now that she had come up to her room so she could watch the village, in case anyone else came to cause trouble, but she fell asleep. Orangino seemed to have taken over sentry duty. She stretched her arms over her head and he turned to look at her, his inscrutable feline face as serene and knowing as ever. Behind him, the sky was turning the orange of sunset. Tomorrow morning she could go out.

"I must have slept for hours," Brianna said. Orangino looked at her knowingly. Then he turned back to gazing out at the village, his ears twitching slightly. Brianna rose and moved to the small window opening behind him. If anyone was out there, they wouldn't be able to see her since the room was in darkness. "Is everything all right?" she whispered, stroking the cat's orange fur. Orangino purred loudly, enjoying the attention, but never moving his gaze from the window. Brianna's stomach growled. When had she last eaten? Had Andera prepared something for her? That had been hours ago! She rubbed her shoulders and climbed down the ladder to the kitchen, followed by the cat, who jumped from the loft floor to a ledge against the wall before landing on the floor.

A soft light glowed in the kitchen, although no lamp burned. The table was set for one, with a white linen cloth and delicate light blue china plates and silver cutlery that Brianna had never seen before. She and her mother had certainly never owned anything so fine. Orangino rubbed against her leg and meowed. It was then that Brianna noticed the note on the counter.

"Orangino's food is in the blue crock on the second shelf. Please give him half a scoop morning and night. And keep it put away between times because he is a bit of a pig. Enjoy your own dinner!"

It was signed "Andera"

Brianna fed the cat, who lapped appreciatively at what looked like fish stew. She wondered where her own dinner was. When she looked back at the table, she noticed another blue crockery bowl, similar to the one that held Orangino's food. Was it there before? It must have been. She lifted the lid and a tantalizing aroma teased her nostrils and made her stomach growl even more.

She sat down at the table, and after a moment of thanks to the spirit that allowed her to have this magical food, she spooned the savory mixture onto her plate. It was a stew of some sort, loaded with vegetables and chunks of a meat she did not recognize, but so tender it fell apart on her fork. She ate hungrily but slowly, as she had been taught, and finally wiped her plate with a slice of the warm bread that rested in a basket wrapped in a white linen towel. How did the bread stay warm? More magic – she knew. Andera – and her mother – were taking care of her.

It was dark out now. But after sleeping all afternoon, Brianna was not tired at all. In fact, she was full of energy. Andera had told her to appreciate the night, to use the silence to make her own magic strong. Orangino reached his front paws up and Brianna made room for him on her lap. He jumped up and settled himself and allowed her to stroke his orange fur. He had been here less than a day, but already she knew that his company and the magic he possessed would save her from loneliness, if nothing else. And she hoped there would be nothing else she needed to be saved from.

The light in the kitchen dimmed, and then went dark. Did this mean it was time to go back upstairs? Brianna had no control over the light, and Orangino still sat calmly on her lap, enjoying her hand on his coat, so she waited. All was silent except for the cat's purring and the faint sound of insects chirping outdoors.

There was a knock at the door, soft at first, like an animal scratching, but then louder and clearly a knock. Brianna jumped, but with the cat firmly on her lap, she did not get up. The knock came again, more insistent. She took a deep breath, preparing to call out, "Who is it?" when Orangino stood on her lap, placing his front paws gently but firmly on her lips. She let out the breath. "Okay," she whispered to the cat. "Okay. I won't say anything, but what am I going to do?"

She heard Andera's voice in her mind. *As long as you stay in the house, you will be safe.* All right. She trusted the magic. But she was curious. What if she just peeked out the window? As long as she knew she was safe, what harm would it do? But she would have to eject the cat from her lap, and she knew he would object as any cat would. She would wait. More pounding on the door. "Hey, witch! Come out!" It was a masculine voice, but a young voice. Brianna breathed in, trying to calm her heartbeat. There was a rumble of more voices, but the words were indistinct.

"I'm safe. I'm safe," she repeated the words to herself like a mantra. In the quiet of the night, thunder rumbled in the distance. *Maybe it will storm and send them away*, she thought. But it was too distant. They had plenty of time to cause trouble.

A flash! But it wasn't lightning. They had lit a fire outside her window. With the light of the fire she could see three young men she had known years ago when she went to the village school. They crouched around the fire, making sure it caught, until lightning flashed and rain began to pour down, dousing the fire and sending the three dashing out of her yard for a safer haven. In the last flash Brianna thought she saw what it was they were attempting to burn. It looked like her mother's basket that she carried with her on the day she left so long ago.

It was a long night. Thunder rumbled from the sea and across the fens – and it rained. The rain poured down in a drenching deluge, then eased to a fine drizzle, but it didn't stop completely until dawn, when the sky cleared and the sun gleamed on the wet land, allowing the villagers to begin the process of drying out themselves and their belongings.

Brianna looked out on a changed world. She and Orangino had sat upstairs in her loft all night, watching the storm and waiting for intruders. They both knew it was very unlikely that anyone would return in a rainstorm, but one never knew. Brianna was certain that her mother's basket would be a sodden mess by morning, and her heart cried for it, but there was nothing she could do. She could not go out in a thunderstorm, and she knew she was not allowed out of the house. If the presence of the basket was a test of her obedience, she had passed the test. Nevertheless, she wondered. How had the boys acquired her mother's basket? It had been months since she had gone. Had they had it all this time? Surely they wouldn't have waited to taunt her with it. Equally mysterious was the presence in the remnants of the basket of something that sparkled, like a jewel. In a few hours she could leave the house and investigate.

Chapter 4

"What you're missing is that the path itself changes you."

Julien Smith, *The Finch*

The basket was ruined. Brianna's eyes filled with tears as she poked at the soggy, charred remnants, woven by her mother's own hands. She recalled her mother carrying the basket over her arm as they walked through the village and into the woods to gather herbs. She could almost hear the sound of her mother's laughter as they walked. But there was something else. As a child Brianna had seen her mother as carefree and fun. But now from the perspective of the years, and the distance of being alone, Brianna remembered a sadness and frustration in her mother's actions that her childish self, had not noticed. Her mother always seemed to be on edge. She was always surveying her surroundings with quick glances. Brianna thought now that her mother was looking for danger. It was no secret that the two of them were disliked by the villagers. No matter how much they tried to behave as their neighbors did, Brianna's mother just could not hide their uniqueness. They were different, and difference was suspect.

The ground was muddy after the storm, and Brianna's thin shoes squished in the wet ground, chilling her feet. She would clean them later and set them in the warm sun to dry. Picking up the basket with her two hands, she thought that she would carry it to the woods and scatter the pieces on the ground. The basket came from nature and would go back to nature. Her mother would love that idea. As her eyes brimmed again with unshed tears, she thought she saw the sparkle in the basket that she had noticed the night before, as if something within the wet material caught the rays of the sun. Everything seemed to sparkle this morning after the storm, but this was different. She blinked, allowing the tears to fall onto the basket, and then she saw it. Buried within the cords of the basket were three gems, one red, one green, and one yellow. Holding her breath, Brianna picked them out with her fingers and held them in her hand. Had they always been there, stuck between the grasses of the basket as her mother carried it about on her errands? Or was it magic -- magic brought by Andera, the spell, and the storm of the night before? She heard voices nearby -- a neighbor with her children whom she knew slightly. Quickly Brianna slipped the gems into the pocket of her skirt and continued into the forest, where she scattered the pieces of her mother's basket on the ground, taking care to pull the fragments apart so the birds would easily be able to carry them in their beaks.

Her task completed, she wiped her eyes with the hem of her skirt. As soon as she reached the edge of the forest, she saw that Graina, the village woman whose voice she heard, was standing in front of her cottage, just on the spot where the basket had lain. Her young twins had spotted Orangino and were trying to catch him, but the savvy cat had taken refuge on a low branch of the apple tree that stood in front of the cottage. He was just out of the children's reach, and he sat crouched looking down with the superiority only a cat can display.

The woman's eyes were on Brianna as she walked towards her. "Brianna, you must leave the village." The woman smiled sadly and took a step closer to Brianna. "This news comes as no surprise, does it? I don't want to see you hurt. I have children of my own, and I know ..." Her voice trailed off. "It's not your fault. I don't believe any of the rumors, but now that your mother has disappeared, it just isn't safe."

"No, of course not. I know I must go." Brianna straightened her shoulders and willed strength into her voice. "I think I have known it since it was clear that Mother wasn't coming back." Tears brimmed again in her eyes. She had known all along that she could not remain in the village indefinitely, but the days had passed since her mother's departure and nothing seemed to change, only her sense of loneliness and isolation increased, along with the growing animosity of most of the villagers. There were a few who were kind and looked out for her as well as they could, but the more they helped her, the more they placed themselves in danger. Brianna knew this day would come.

Graina took Brianna's hand in hers. "I think you are stronger than you were, and you know where to go, and what you must do. Am I right, Brianna?"

Brianna felt the teardrops coursing down her cheeks as she answered, "Yes." She thought of her mother, and then of Andera and lastly of Orangino, the cat who did not speak, but guided her just the same.

"I must tell you what the priest said." Graina's voice was barely a whisper.

A small cloud passed in front of the sun, and Brianna shivered. If the village priest was speaking of her, she was in more danger than she thought. She clenched her fists at her sides as she tried to control her emotions.

"You know he feels threatened by the old beliefs."

"What did he say?" Brianna's voice was barely audible above the pounding of her heart.

"He said you are a witch, just like your mother. And you should be burned, as she should have been if she had not used her demonic powers to disappear."

Brianna rubbed her arms. When she touched the star tattoo, she felt its heat. This was worse than she had imagined. "My mother's powers are not demonic."

"I know that. Most of the village knows that, but they dare not speak out. The church is too powerful. He will have the soldiers on us." The woman studied Brianna's face. "Do you know where you will go?"

"I'll follow my mother," Brianna answered with a firm voice, a voice that hid the fear she felt.

"But do you know where she has gone?"

"No. Not exactly. But I have – help."

Graina's twins had given up trying to catch Orangino, who still sat on his branch, watching Brianna intently as if he understood every word of the conversation, which of course he did. The children had found some sticks and were using them to dig in the soft earth where the basket had been, a harmless enough pastime.

Graina nodded. "When will you go?"

"By morning. I'll be gone by morning," Brianna said. "It's better that way. You can say you didn't see me, and you don't know where I've gone."

Clouds had moved across the sun, and a chill wind began to blow in from the sea. Graina called her children, and before she left she touched Brianna's cheek with her hand. "You will be all right," she whispered.

Chapter 5

She took a step and didn't want to take any more, but she did."

Markus Zusak, *The Book Thief*

Brianna spent the day remembering. It was the only way she could prevent herself from being afraid about the future. She wished Andera would come back. She had made up her mind to leave in the morning, and she knew Orangino would be with her, but how much could a cat do if someone accused her of witchcraft? She had to trust herself, to follow her intuition and take one step at a time on her journey out of the village. Somehow she would be safe. She had to be. Surely if she were in serious danger Andera would return.

When she closed the cottage door as darkness fell, Orangino investigated every corner of the two simple rooms, reassuring himself and Brianna that all was well. He then curled up on the chair closest to the fire and went to sleep, which Brianna took as a sign that she should go to sleep as well. She planned to be up before daylight. As she gazed around the house that had been her only home, she felt a bitter sweetness that brought tears to her eyes again, but it was time to move on. The time for tears was done. She blinked them away before climbing up to her loft room, where she lay down on her bed and fell asleep.

Her rest was short and fitful. Her dreams were populated with the faces of people she had known all her life. Her mother was there, trying to reassure her daughter that everything would be all right. But how could that be? Her mother was gone. There was the face of the village priest. He seemed a nice enough man, if you attended Mass on Sunday and had your children baptized. Brianna had never been baptized; her mother refused to even consider it. She had seen the priest playing with the children as they kicked a ball in the street, but when Brianna and her mother approached, he called the children away, making the sign against the evil eye. If he wasn't superstitious, and didn't believe in magic, why did he make the sign? Andera appeared in her dream along with her mother. The two seemed to be mixed up together, one and the same. And of course Orangino. Once she woke and saw the orange cat on the window sill, staring out at the moonlit night, watching, guarding. It comforted Brianna to know he was there.

Sometime before dawn, the cat rubbed against her, waking her up. If it were a normal day, she would have thought he was hungry, or wanted to go outside, but this was different. It was time to go. "Are you coming with me, Orangino? I really need a familiar face. I honestly don't know where I'm going. I need you to show me the way." The cat rubbed hard against her legs, purring loudly.

Brianna dressed quickly. She took her mother's extra shawl from the hook where it had been hanging since she left. As she wrapped it around her shoulders, her mother's scent rose from the fabric, causing a pang of loneliness that frightened the young girl. She moved quickly to pack some bread and cheese and a couple of apples. There was nothing else. She would have to trust that she would find food along the way. As she looked around the small cottage one last time, she saw nothing else that mattered. Maybe she would return, with or without her mother, or maybe not. As she checked to be sure the fire was out -- it certainly wouldn't do to have the house burn down -- Brianna noticed something gleaming on the floor. Orangino waited patiently by the door, but Brianna bent to check. It was a coin -- not gold, only silver -- but something that might help her in the days to come. Without questioning where the coin had come from, Brianna slipped it into the tiny pocket in the hem of her skirt where she had hidden the gems from her mother's basket.

It was time to go. Brianna opened the door to the dim pre-dawn light. Orangino slipped out ahead of her and sauntered to the gate. She silently opened the latch and the two of them were on the road.

"There she is!" A child's voice hissed in the darkness, causing Brianna's heart to stop. Was she not to escape after all?

Then a soft feminine voice which Brianna recognized as Graina who had visited the day before, called out, "It's all right, Brianna. You can trust us. We are on our way to Newark to the market, and you can travel with us."

Brianna had not dared to think how she -- a young girl of thirteen -- would travel alone, when she didn't even know her destination. But Newark was a good destination, at least to start. In the dim light she saw the family. They had always been kind to her and her mother, although somewhat distant. "We aren't known to be your friends, Brianna. And that will only make it safer for all of us," Graina's husband Roger said.

A boy a couple of years younger than Brianna stood holding a cow by its bridle. The twins, who had chased Orangino the day before, tried to copy the confident stance of their brother and father, but succeeded only in elbowing their brother in the ribs. He scowled and moved away.

"This is Anna, children," Graina said. "She will be traveling with us." When Brianna looked at her with the question in her eyes, the woman added softly, "It's better that way. In case anyone asks questions or is looking for you."

Orangino moved into the circle and rubbed against Brianna's legs. "This is my cat," she said. "He will follow along but he isn't any trouble. He finds his own food." "Yes, I noticed him yesterday." The woman looked at Brianna with an even gaze. She knew everything. But Brianna had no choice but to trust the family. Orangino, or even Andera, would surely have let her know if this were a trap.

Chapter 6

"A good traveler has no fixed plans and is not intent on arriving."

Lao Tzu

"We need to get moving," Roger announced. "It will be light soon. The farther we are from the village at first light, the better off we will be. We have a cow to sell, and if we are first at the market, we may be able to sell her and start back early." He winked at Brianna.

The little group moved off down the road. It was still chilly, and Brianna was glad of her mother's shawl wrapped around her shoulders. The father and older boy led the way with the cow, which seemed glad enough to be out for a stroll, followed by the twins holding tightly to each other's hands, and Brianna and the mother brought up the rear. Orangino moved in and out of the group, although no one paid any attention to him except for Brianna. Once he was gone from sight so long that Brianna began to think he was lost, but then he appeared from the brush at the side of the road, licking his whiskers. Apparently he had found a small rodent or bird to serve as his breakfast.

As the sun grew brighter, the family began to see other groups traveling the same road. Newark-on-Trent attracted a large crowd on market days. Once a troop of horsemen passed traveling in the opposite direction. The small groups of peasants moved well off the road to allow them to pass.

The horses traveled at great speed, leaving a cloud of dust. "I wonder where they are going? There is nothing that direction but small villages like ours," the oldest boy said, as he held tight to the rope that served as the cow's bridle.

"The king was said to be traveling in this part of the country," his father replied. "Mayhap it has something to do with that. Not our business, certainly. Except to stay out of their way."

They moved on, and as the road became more crowded, the father decided it was time to pause and break their fast before entering the hubbub of the town. When they came across a busy inn on the outskirts of Newark, they stopped. The boy tethered the cow to a tree and sat cross-legged on the ground, glad enough to rest his legs, but not about to leave the precious animal, which would likely fetch enough to see the family through the winter. "I'll go in for some cider, and find out what news there is." Roger strode off in the direction of the inn.

The rest of the group arranged themselves on the ground, and Graina pulled oatcakes from her satchel and passed them around to her children. She started to hand one to Brianna, who was just removing her own food from her bag. "No thank you. I brought my own." As she pulled out an apple, she saw the twins eyeing the fruit. "If you have a knife, I would be happy to share."

"Thank you," the mother said, removing a small but sharp knife from her bag. "The children don't have treats like that often." As she handed the knife to Brianna, she added, "You must take an oatcake in return. You may need it later."

Brianna agreed and wrapped the cake in the cloth with her other food. "I'm grateful."

They had begun to eat their shared food when Roger emerged from the inn, carrying a small jug in his hand. "It's a job getting through the crowd in there, all clamoring for the latest gossip. And there is news of the king." He took a swig of the cider from the jug and handed it to his wife.

Everyone, including the children, looked up at his words. News of the king could affect all of them, especially since they were on the road away from their home village. "His treasure has been lost." Everyone in the group gaped at him, unable to absorb his words. The king's treasure lost? Did that mean he was no longer king? The nobles were powerful, it was true, and would like to see him gone, but how could his treasure be lost? Had they stolen it? "It seems the king came ahead to St. Mary's Abbey at Swineshead to spend some nights there with a few of his noblemen. The rest of his train, including the wagon containing the Crown Jewels, was lost in the Wash." Everyone who lived in this part of England was familiar with the Wash, the soggy arm of the North Sea that jutted inland, creating an obstacle to anyone traveling north along the coast, especially a group as unwieldy as the king's entourage. But King John's men were not stupid. Surely they would know the schedule of the tides.

"And the rest of the King's men?" Brianna asked. "And the rest of the wagons in the train? Were they all lost?"

"I don't know," he answered. "All the talk is of the treasure. All the jewels that have belonged to the kings of England since the time of Edward the Confessor and before. All gone." He took another sip of cider and cleared his throat before continuing. "There's more."

"How can there be more that is worse than this?" his wife asked. "The King will be angry. There is already anger between the King and his nobles, after they made him sign that agreement at Runnymede. Not that it did us any good, but the nobles seemed satisfied with themselves."

Her husband glanced around to be sure no one heard his wife's last comment. It was true -- the nobles in England were becoming quite powerful. It was the first time anyone knew of when a group of nobles had forced a king to sign an agreement with them, an agreement that gave them unheard of rights in the realm. But it was also true that the Magna Carta, as it was called, had little if any effect on the lives of the peasants. "The King is ill," Roger said quietly. "Dying, some say." One of the twins started to say something, but his father held his finger to his lips. "I know nothing but what I hear. And it is best we don't speak of it." Brianna handed the cider jug back to him and he drained the last of it, before swallowing the last chunk of bread that he had held in his hand as he spoke. "It is best -- I think -- that we move on to the market and see if we can sell this beast." He lowered his voice again and the group bent in to hear him. "If anything happens to the King, the market will likely be closed in mourning. I have no wish to walk back to the village with a cow in tow."

Brianna touched the hem of her skirt, rubbing it between her fingers. The gems she had found in her mother's basket felt hot, almost burning her skin. They couldn't be some of the King's gems, supposed to be lost in the Wash? Impossible! But what was impossible?

The family got to their feet and prepared to move on. "I will leave you when we reach the market," Brianna announced.

"But where will you go?" Graina's brow was creased with concern.

"I'll find my way," Brianna started to add something more when Orangino rubbed against her skirts, just where her hand had been moments before when she felt the gem hidden there. He meowed plaintively, staring up at his mistress.

Roger and Graina both looked uneasy, their eyes meeting above the children's heads, but Brianna knew. It was best, for the sake of their family, if she was gone. The story of someone associated with witchcraft could follow them even away from their home village. And the King's illness and possible death could throw the entire region into turmoil.

"I'll find work as a kitchen maid." Brianna held her chin high with confidence. "I'll be all right."

"Very well then," Graina shouldered her bag, lighter now that they had eaten. "Let's walk."

The crowds grew more and more intense as they approached the town. Brianna saw no reason for a formal farewell, since it was clear to all that she needed to leave for the safety of the family. She noticed that Orangino was staying close by her side, more like a dog than a cat, and she knew it was for her safety, not his. They were stopped once by soldiers demanding their business in the town. When it was clear that they were no more than a peasant family traveling to market with their cow, they were allowed to move on. Brianna realized that Orangino had hidden beneath her skirts while Roger spoke with the soldiers.

When they moved into the thickest of the crowds near the market, Brianna knew it was time. Without a word, she moved away from the family who had helped her. In less than a minute she was out of their sight.

Chapter 7

"All happiness depends on courage and work."

Honoré de Balzac

Brianna took care to keep her head low and concentrate on not being seen as she made her way through the market crowds. She would find the kitchen entrance of a large household and offer her help. She could clean pots in exchange for a bit of food and a place to sleep to start out with, and then show her abilities and her worth. She heard people speaking of the King, but she did not stop long enough to hear the latest news. The turmoil in the streets was to her advantage now. She intended to find work and then figure out her next move.

She elbowed her way out of the throng around the main square where the market was held and turned into a side street. She wanted to find the townhouse of a noble or rich merchant, one where the servants were busy preparing food for the great numbers of guests who would be lodging there because of the king's visit. Someone, the cook or the housekeeper, would put her to work without asking many questions, happy to have two more hands and two more feet to help with the work. She raised her head and pretended that she knew where she was going, that she was on an important errand for her mistress and dare not tarry. Occasionally she caught a glimpse of Orangino making his way across the roofs that overhung the street. He leapt effortlessly from house to house, his route parallel to that of his mistress.

The street she had chosen was filled with activity. Brianna walked purposefully past one townhouse that had soldiers milling about. She didn't want to be hassled or asked uncomfortable questions. The second townhouse looked more promising. It was larger than the first and just as busy, but the comings and goings were more those of servants on their daily errands than military men. She walked in through the open gate and headed for the kitchen entrance. Her guess was confirmed when she smelled bread baking, reminding her stomach of her meager breakfast. But she paused and almost walked back to the street when she heard the crash of crockery and the cry of an oath. "God's blood, girl! Is there no one as clumsy as you? Get out. Go back to your whore of a mother, if she'll have you. I won't have you! Now out!"

A girl about Brianna's age stumbled out of the door, nearly tripping over Orangino, who had just landed on the ground in a graceful crouch. Brianna expected to see the girl in tears, but her small round face held an anger that was frightening. "Who are you?" she asked when she saw Brianna.

"I'm Brianna. I'm looking for work. But this doesn't seem to be a good time."

"Oh, it's a good time, all right, since I just got the sack. She'll be glad enough to have you until you break something. The first time she'll only beat you." The girl wiped her runny nose on her dirty sleeve, which was worn to the point of colorlessness.

"I don't want to take your job."

"Yes, you do. I can see it in your eyes. And someone has to. If not you, it will be some other girl. Go on, but I'll be back, and you will help me kill her."

"I . . ." Brianna was shocked; she had no intention of killing anyone. She had nothing against the cook, at least not yet. And even if she did, she knew murderers would hang, even a girl as young as she.

The girl laughed. "Afraid, are you? Just be my eyes and ears. I'll be back." The girl gave Brianna a strange look. Her eyes seemed to grow older, and for a moment she appeared to grow taller, like a grown woman, before she disappeared into the crowded street.

Brianna watched her go, and then quickly shook herself out of her trance and adopted a swaggering walk to the door of the kitchen, where she could see a boy still cleaning up the broken crockery and some oily liquid that had been spilled.

A tall, stout woman with brown hair turning to gray stood over him with a hefty wooden paddle in her hand. "Now get a brush and soap and water and scrub the floor. I won't have people slipping and falling and ruining more food." Her quick eyes took in Brianna at the door.

"Who are you?" This was the second person at this house who had greeted her with that perfunctory question.

"My name is Brianna. I'm a cook's maid looking for work."

The woman narrowed her eyes at the newcomer, as if that would give her information into her background and character. "Well, come on then. I don't have time to chat with you. You sleep in the corner there." She pointed to a pile of straw in an alcove at the end of the room, just behind the door where Brianna stood. "You eat what you are given. Now go with this one . . ." She pointed to a skinny girl about Brianna's age who stood hopping back and forth from one foot to another. " . . . and bring up a bushel of apples from the cellar. And watch her. Don't let her pee on the floor. Cuff her if she does and tell me."

Brianna took the other handle of the basket held by the hopping girl. "Why don't you go outside or to the privy?"

"Because she won't let me. She says I go too much and I'm just trying to get out of work."

37

"Let's hurry and get the apples then." Brianna wondered if she would be treated the same way, or if the cook would find some other way to torture her.

The girl, whose name was Alice, managed to control herself until they returned to the kitchen with the basket of apples, but then she ran from the kitchen. The cook seemed to have forgotten about Alice-who-pees-too-much, at least for the moment. She took the basket of apples from Brianna, who had struggled to carry it across the room after the other girl ran to the privy. The older woman easily lifted the heavy basket over her head and placed it on a work table against the far wall. Brianna shuddered to think of the feel of a wooden paddle in that woman's hands. She planned to keep her eyes open for the first opportunity to move out of this kitchen to a better situation.

"You know how to cut apples, little miss dreamer?"

"Yes, ma'am." Brianna snapped to attention.

"I'm not a ma'am." The reprimand from the cook came swiftly. "That is what you call the lady of the house, if you should ever meet her, and let's pray you don't until you learn what you are doing here. I am 'Cook.' That's all you need to know."

"Yes, Cook."

"Now, you say you know how to cut apples. Do you have a knife?"

"No, ma'am -- Cook."

Cook's gaze surveyed the kitchen and the people working under her supervision. "Lia, where is that knife left here by that little . . ." Her sentence went unfinished.

"It's here some place," The woman called Lia, who was rolling out pastry crust, wiped the sweat from her forehead with the back of her hand and looked around. She frowned when she saw the knife, its point buried into the wood next to the door leading down to the cellar. "Now what is it doing there?" Lia pulled the knife from the wall and handed it handle first to Cook.

Brianna was sure the knife had not been there when she and Alice went down for the apples, nor was it there when they returned. Brianna watched as Cook tested the blade with her thumb. "Not sharp enough to kill a man, but sharp enough for apples." She handed the knife to Brianna. "Let's see if you can cut apples. And waste no time. With Lord Alfred and his lady dining here tonight with his brother from London, we have no time to play."

Brianna accepted the knife and tested the blade against her own thumb. Then she ran her forefinger along the design on the hilt. This was no kitchen knife. It was a dagger, finally honed in Toledo in Spain. The black design in the metal identified it. But the swirls in the design looked Celtic, with their intertwining circles. Her mother had a similar knife long ago. She reached for an apple and began to peel, halve, quarter, core and slice the apples, as she had been taught by her mother. She had finished about a dozen when Alice was put to work next to her, but she was slower and less precise in her slicing. It made Brianna look good, she knew, but she hated to see Alice stumbling about, and she was worried that the girl might slice her hand. "Hold your fingers this way." She demonstrated how she held the fingertips on her left hand curved inward. "This way there is less danger of cutting yourself, and if you do, it will be a small nick, not a cut that can bleed all over the apples."

Alice was still slow, but she looked gratefully at Brianna. At least she was not incurring the wrath of Cook. The woman checked on the two girls, ready to criticize, but there was nothing for her to say but "Humph!" When they had finished, Brianna had no more than a minute to rub her cramped fingers before she was called. "New girl! What is your name?"

"Brianna."

"Yes, Brianna. Go with Robert here. We need more fish for tonight."

"Yes, Cook."

Robert was a few years younger than Brianna, and she had never seen a dirtier person, except for the beggars lying in the gutter. She wondered that Cook allowed him around the kitchen. While they walked toward the market, Brianna asked, "Have you worked here long?"

He snorted. "You might say all my life. The woman you call Cook is my mother." Brianna stared. "And before you ask, I'm not always this dirty. I'm being punished."

"You are being punished by being covered with dirt?"

"I fell yesterday. In the muck. I went to see the King's horses and I fell. I wasn't supposed to be there, and when she found out, she said I can't wash for a week." They were in the thick of the crowd now. Brianna wondered if Roger and his family were still in Newark, or if they had sold their cow and returned to the village.

"So the King is staying nearby?" Brianna had to shout over the noise of the throng, as she struggled to keep up with the boy.

"He is. Just two houses down on the other side of the road. Lord Alfred is host to several of his nobles. That is why we are so swamped with work, cooking for all these people."

Brianna was trying to absorb this information, figure out if it had anything to do with her, and keep close to Robert when they reached the market place. "The fish seller is this way." Robert pointed and headed to the left, Brianna close behind.

They had almost reached their destination when there was a commotion just ahead of them. A knight mounted on a gigantic horse stood shouting at someone. Robert grabbed Brianna's arm and pulled her around so they could see what was going on. It was obvious that Robert was attracted to trouble and chaos like a magnet to iron. The knight's page had a small boy by the scruff of his neck, and Brianna was horrified to see that the boy was one of the twins from the village. But where was the rest of his family? She moved up closer now, with Robert at her side.

"This boy has tried to steal my purse," the knight shouted. "I'll have him beaten."

Where could his parents be? wondered Brianna. She was sure they would not leave him to a fate like this, even though there was little they could do about the situation. At least they would be there, pleading for their boy. Perhaps they had somehow become separated in the crowd.

"He didn't steal it!" An older child's voice cried out.

"And who might you be?" bellowed the knight. Brianna studied the man on horseback. He was an older knight, who had probably seen many battles in service of the king. His hair and beard were as much gray as brown, and a scar crossed his cheek. It was faded now, but it must have been a painful wound when it happened.

"I'm his brother." The boy's voice faltered, but Brianna could see the relief in his little brother's face.

"Then why did he have my purse in his hands?" added the knight in the same loud voice. The fracas had attracted a crowd as to a street show, and they cleared a space around the participants.

"I don't know. Maybe it fell and he was returning it to you." The crowd roared with laughter, and the boy's words were repeated to those standing further back in the crowd. This was going to be good.

The little boy looked pleadingly up at the knight, tears streaming down his face. Then he saw Brianna and his eyes lit in recognition. Brianna's heart stopped. There was little if anything she could do to help. But the knight saw the direction of the boy's gaze, and by this time the older boy had seen her as well. The knight turned his horse, its hooves moving dangerously near Brianna's feet. "You girl!" The knight's full attention was now directed at her, and he narrowed his eyes, showing the wrinkles that surrounded them. "Do you know these thieving boys? They seem to know you. Have you put them up to this? Maybe you are here to collect your share of my coins?" Brianna heard Robert, standing next to her, gasp in shock. Maybe he was drawn to trouble, but this was too dangerous even for his taste.

Brianna took a deep breath. The truth. "I traveled with them from my village, but we are not thieves. I work in the kitchen of Lord Alfred." The tattoo on her arm had begin to itch, but she dared not look at it.

"Do you now? It seems I am going there now, so we will find out."

Someone touched Brianna's shoulder. Thinking it was someone in the crowd, she moved in the opposite direction. The hand tightened on her shoulder. Trouble. Brianna turned to see the face of her magical aunt Andera. She winked at Brianna, and then turned her gaze back to the knight, whose face was still suffused with anger as he looked around him. He drew in a breath to speak, but the words never left his mouth. A black dog raced through the crowd, barely avoiding the forelegs of the knight's charger, followed by a familiar looking orange cat. The horse reared in fright, nearly unseating the knight. Brianna saw the two boys from the village take the opportunity and run through the crowd. Robert grabbed her hand. "Let's get out of here. Cook will kill us!"

As he pulled her toward their destination in the market, Brianna craned her neck for another look at Andera, but the woman was gone, as were the dog and the cat. She realized that she had not seen Orangino since she began work in the kitchen, but he must have been nearby, as was Andera. They were watching out for her, but what was next? The knight would not forget her face.

Cook was standing at the door, her arms akimbo, when Robert and Brianna returned with the basket of fish. "You're back! And none too soon. I heard there was trouble in the square. You too weren't involved, were you?"

"No, ma'm." Robert answered before Brianna could open her mouth.

"You better not be." She looked from one to the other but said nothing more about their lateness. "Put the basket on the table. There is more work to be done."

As she returned to her work at the hearth, Cook announced to no one in particular. "The king is ill. Some say he is dying, but his men still want their meals." The rest of the kitchen help either already knew, or they didn't care. What difference did the death of a king make to people such as they? Their lives continued as always. They cooked, ran errands, cleaned in the houses of their "betters." If anything, there was more work when something momentous happened. And to have it happen when the king was visiting Newark created even more tasks for the servants. Brianna threw herself into the work of carrying bowls of food from one place to another, running errands to the cellar, and generally staying out of everyone else's way. When the meal was finally served in the early afternoon, she took a moment to step outside. The air of the town was smoky and foul. She wondered if it was like this all the time. She missed the fresh air of the village, where she could see the clouds and watch the passage of the sun from horizon to horizon. Here there were only the narrow walls of the street. But she didn't plan to stay here forever. This was only the first stage of her journey. Andera's presence in the town square today had proven that Brianna was safe and was being guided. She stood thinking, oblivious of all that was around here, when she heard a shout, "There she is!"

The boy was about her age, and dressed in the livery of a page. Brianna slipped back into the kitchen. The

43

commotion had calmed somewhat while the noblemen and their ladies ate their dinner, but serving maids still went to and fro between the kitchen and dining hall. "Is there anything I can do to help?" she asked. The rest of the kitchen staff looked at her strangely. No one ever asked that. You simply waited to be told what to do, and the orders came soon enough.

"Here," called one of the serving maids. "Help me carry this." Brianna gratefully took one side of a heavy platter laden with vegetables and went through into the dining hall.

The room was vast and dark, lit by candles even in the afternoon. The smells of cooked food made Brianna's stomach grumble, as she realized she had not eaten since early in the morning. She tried to look around at the people enjoying the feast -- it was her first opportunity to see the nobles of the kingdom, but the serving girl walked quickly, and Brianna had to keep up if she didn't want to cause a spill.

As they set down the platter just one table down from that of the lord and his lady, Brianna sensed someone looking at her. She glanced up to meet the eyes of the knight from the town square. He said nothing, but his eyes never left her face.

Chapter 8

"The most precious etchings of caring can be traced not in the scope of its message, but in the integrity of its purpose."

Johnathan Jena

Lincoln Castle
Magic Realm

Andera waited for her father, the great wizard Jonathan, to look up. She had been trained since childhood to respect the work of more powerful magicians, and her father was one of the most powerful. Andera had inherited his strength of character and ability to concentrate, as well as a prodigious memory, making her an esteemed worker of magic in her own right, but still she waited for her father to acknowledge her presence. He sat at his desk, a large oak piece that required six men, or the wave of a magic wand, to move it. Her mother tried to polish it from time to time, but no matter how much precious lemon oil she used, or how many incantations she spoke employing the words "shine," "gleam," or "glow," it still retained a certain dull shabbiness. Andera sensed that he liked it that way. She was pondering these thoughts along with affectionate ones for both her parents, when he set his quill pen in a pot of ink and looked up at his daughter.

"So," he began with a smile. "You and your mother have given up trying to bring a shine to my desk as well as to me. And you have been to Newark to rescue my granddaughter from her encounter with Sir Michael."

"Yes, sir." She always used the title "sir" with him, although he did not require it.

"And she has found the knife, or rather it has been given to her." Jonathan stared out the high window opening for a moment, resting his eyes and thinking as clouds scudded across the blue sky. "A storm is coming." He turned back to his daughter. "A storm is coming in more ways than one. In the physical world, I see rain and wind. But any mortal can read the signs of nature. I also see a storm in the lives of the men and women of England. King John will die, providing an opportunity for his nobles to compete for the power to control young Prince Henry."

Andera knew these things as well as her father. As magic folk, they could not control the overall greed and selfishness that plagued humanity, they could only live among mortals from time to time and exert their influence on a few individuals who chose to listen, or, as in the case of King John's treasure, teach a lesson. Andera spoke. "Mara, the kitchen maid who was given the sack by the cook, has gone. She left the knife behind, just as we asked her to."

"She is one of us," Jonathan replied. "Although only half magic on her mother's side, she will have recognized something in Brianna. But her anger was stronger at that moment than her sense of magic. Fortunately, Brianna has the knife now, and I sense that she knows it wasn't given to her by accident."

Andera opened her mouth to speak when something shifted in the atmosphere. Both father and daughter felt it, and their eyes met through the shimmering air. The shift was strong. In the world of mortals it had the strength of a minor earthquake. In the magic world, it caused the air to vibrate in such a way that it set their teeth on edge. "Nothing that strong brings good," Andera whispered.

"You are right," her father replied. "I must determine where it came from." He rose from his seat and went to the fireplace where small flames danced, just enough to take the chill off the castle room. He reached his hand into the air above his head and produced a small vial of a sparkly blue powder. Muttering an incantation for knowledge, Jonathan tossed the contents of the vial on the flames, causing a crackling and a loud whoosh as the flames shot up the chimney. When they settled again, blue sparks continued to rise and subside in the orange blaze. Jonathan and Andera read the message in the flames. Each spark, by its intensity and location, and the speed of its rise and fall, appeared like words on parchment to father and daughter. "King John is dead, and England has a child for a king," Jonathan read.

"This will bring peace to England for a time. That is good news." Andera glanced at her father, who continued to study the flames.

"There is more. Kings die and their sons are crowned all the time in the mortal world. And the peace never lasts. That is why we are here." He pulled his wand, tipped with amber which glowed golden in the light of the fire, from his voluminous sleeve and waved it in a figure eight. The flames jumped and the blue sparks flew, some of them escaping the hearth to hover above the heads of Jonathan and Andera before turning to ash. "This message was sent by Rowena, the witch of Guildford." They watched the message in the sparks together.

"Rowena is dying," Andera said softly. "She knows she has not long to live among mortals. But we were counting on her to train Brianna. And Guildford is far, south of London. Can we use magic to carry Brianna to Rowena's village?"

"Decidedly not. It is important that Brianna make her own way. She has spent too little time on her own to be prepared to learn what she needs to learn. She has to know why her magic education is important." Again he waved his wand above the flames and waited. "Rowena will live long enough to teach Brianna and influence her in magic ways. I am sure of it."

"How will she travel there?" Andera saw the twinkle in her father's eyes. "You have it all figured out, don't you? You have had it figured out all along."

He nodded his head, causing his long gray locks to fall forward across his brow. "I must get your mother to trim my hair."

"You aren't answering me, father." Andera pulled herself to her full height and looked him in the eye.

"Michael will take her." Her father smiled.

Chapter 9

"In all ages hypocrites, called priests, have put crowns on
the heads of thieves, called kings."

Robert G. Ingersoll

Brianna slept soundly on her pile of straw. Alice and
another girl were next to her, and although Brianna would
have much preferred to be in a comfortable bed by herself,
the two other girls provided much needed body warmth,
especially as the night lengthened toward morning. Alice got
up once, presumably to use the privy, and Brianna sensed
once that Orangino was curled up next to her, but that might
have been a dream. Sometime toward morning, there was the
sound of horses in the street outside, and men shouting, and
soon Cook was waking the sleeping children, telling them it
was time to get up. There was firewood to fetch, bread to
bake, food to be prepared for the meals today. Brianna
rubbed her eyes, smoothed her skirt and went outside. There
was already great activity in the street, and Brianna, who had
never slept in a town before, was struck by the comings and
goings of men on horseback.

Robert emerged from the kitchen and stood next to her,
scratching himself through his still filthy shirt. "What's
going on?" Brianna asked him.

"Don't know. I guess we will find out soon enough. Must
have something to do with the King, since that's the house
where he's staying." He pointed down the street where
several soldiers and noblemen stood conversing in the early
morning light.

"Robert! Brianna! In here! Now!" Cook shouted from the kitchen. "I didn't know you had time to stand on the stoop chatting like fish wives. Robert, get the fire going. Brianna, go into the hall with Alice and pick up any drinking vessels that may be lying around. But don't disturb them that are still sleeping, or there will be hell to pay!" She aimed a kick at Alice's back side.

"She's in a foul mood this morning," Robert muttered. "Or fouler than most mornings."

Brianna followed Alice into the hall to pick up the drinking vessels. There were several men stretched out asleep on the floor, wrapped in cloaks, and even a few still seated with their heads resting on the tables. The girls tiptoed around them, not only from fear of chastisement from Cook, but the last thing they wanted was to wake a sleeping soldier who had undoubtedly drunk too much the night before. They caught each other's eyes and grimaced at the snoring and foul breath that emerged when they moved too close to the sleeping men.

When they returned to the kitchen with the last load of vessels to be washed, they were amazed to see the entire kitchen staff, including Cook, standing speechless.

"The king is dead," Robert whispered to the two girls. They could hear the men in the dining hall rousing and talking among themselves, so someone had brought them the news. They would be wanting food and drink soon, before taking up their jockeying for advantageous positions in the court of the new king, or rather his regents since King John's son and heir was just a child.

"It's means little to us, unless we are told to do something different. People still need to eat, and one king or another makes little difference in the lives of such as us." Cook's voice was considerably softer than her usual shouting, but it carried force just the same. "Let's get to our work, and without gossip and gawking in the street."

Brianna was put to work slicing onions, as she had acquitted herself so well the day before with the apples. Once again she was given the knife from Toledo to use. She dared to ask Robert, "Why am I using this to slice vegetables? It's a dagger, and a valuable one."

He shrugged his shoulders. "It looks ordinary to me," was all he said before his mother pulled him away by the ear and sent him on an errand.

Brianna sharpened the knife as she had seen others do at a whetstone in the corner. The hilt sparkled, sending tiny points of light into the smoky kitchen air, but no one paid it any mind. "I'm the only one who can see it," she whispered to herself. "I'm the only one who knows what this knife is."

She had finished the onions and was wiping the last of the tears from her eyes with her sleeve. Another kitchen maid, not much older than Brianna, handed her a brush and water and told her to scrub the table. "Mind you use salt, but not too much. The salt will get the onion smell out. Otherwise the next apple tarts we make will taste of onion." Brianna sprinkled a bit of salt from the saltbox and got to work. She had done this many times in the village, and knew the truth of the properties of the salt. Absorbed in her work, she did not notice the young page who came to the kitchen door and spoke to Cook.

"Girl! Come here!"

Brianna jumped and almost dropped the scrub brush from her hands.

She walked obediently to the door, and beyond in the street she recognized the knight from the town square the day before. Was there more trouble? Was she being blamed for the theft? Or worse, had something happened to the boys from the village?

"Yes, Cook."

"They need more kitchen help at the house where the King was lodged. God rest his soul. I could really use your help but the King's household comes first."

Brianna retrieved her few belongings from the sleeping corner and returned. Cook straightened the girl's blouse and whispered, "Mind yourself now. I won't be having it said that someone from my kitchen does poor work." The woman looked again at the knight who stood waiting. It was odd that a knight would come searching for kitchen help, but who knew the ways of the nobility.

Chapter 10

"The best lightning rod for your protection is your own spine."

Ralph Waldo Emerson

Brianna had no choice but to walk past the knight on her way to the house where the king had died. She was nearly there when Robert ran up breathlessly behind her. "Take this. You may need it," he whispered, and pressed the dagger she had used to slice apples and onions into her hand.

"But . . ." Before she could say anything else, he was gone. Pretending to scratch her leg, she slipped the knife into her boot. She took a few quick steps and was suddenly face to face with the knight, his tall, muscular figure looming in front of her. He exchanged some words with the men who stood around the entrance, serious expressions on their faces. Whether their grim faces were out of respect for the king or concern at how his death might advance their own political fortunes, was impossible to tell. Brianna didn't care. She had her own future to worry about. Right now, she was being put to work in the house where the King had just died, and had been brought here specifically by a powerful man who might do her harm, or might be her protector, and she had no way of knowing which.

Before her mind could made any further conjectures, the knight turned back to her. "The kitchen door is down there. See that you work well." He winked at her, and Brianna's stomach clenched in fear. She passed down a narrow alley and found the door to the kitchen, easily recognizable by its tantalizing smells and the shouts of the cook. Kitchens were always the same, and at the door to the kitchen sat an unmistakable orange cat, serenely licking his paws, as if he, for one, had enjoyed a good breakfast.

"Orangino?" He looked at her, and then turned his back to continue his grooming.

The kitchen seemed quite the same as the last one, and Brianna was immediately put to work slicing onions again. She was handed a knife to use, not as sharp or as beautiful as the dagger from Toledo, but it did the job. She was simply told that she was responsible for it and to return it to "the knife boy" when she was done. "The knife boy" smirked with superiority, and Brianna scowled at him. She was the new girl again.

The morning passed quickly as the kitchen staff prepared for the mid-day meal. Just as they were about to serve, the butler came in with news. "The King is to be buried in Worcester. The entourage will leave at first light. Some of you will be asked to accompany the royal court to cook and serve meals until after the burial. I will let you know soon who will be chosen."

Brianna worked through the dinner hour in a daze, loading platters and helping to carry them in to the great hall. The diners were subdued, but quiet talk buzzed all around. King John's small son would be the next king, which meant someone would act as regent until he came of age. It would not be his mother, a French woman, so it would surely be one of the knights.

Brianna was relieved to see that the mysterious knight was not at dinner. Enough time had passed that she was no longer worried about the boys from the village. If the authorities were going to arrest the boys for the theft of the purse, it would have happened, and Brianna would have been called in. And the knight certainly knew where she was.

Kathleen Heady

Brianna did not sense danger from the gray-haired knight, but she did sense that he was important to her in some way.

When the dinner was done and the kitchen put back in order, the servants were allowed to eat. Brianna ate a bit of bread and vegetables, but there was too much on her mind for her to have much appetite. She stepped outside for some fresh air. The sun was sinking and already there was a chill in the air between the buildings, so close were they to each other. In the shadows, Brianna thought she saw a large black dog at the end of the street. It loped towards her, but then stopped and turned around and returned to the shadows. The next thing she saw was the bright orange fur of Orangino, strolling casually up the street from the same spot where she had last seen the dog. Strange, Brianna thought. Cats and dogs didn't usually get on that well, but then Orangino was an unusual cat.

Orangino's green eyes glowed, and he headed straight for Brianna. He rubbed himself fiercely against her skirts, making the air crackle with electricity. Small sparks jumped from his fur and dissipated in the cold air. The air felt charged with magic. Brianna bent to stroke the cat, taking energy and calmness from him. A moment passed and her heart jumped. A pair of black boots stood in front of her. She looked up to the half-smiling face of the knight.

Chapter 11

"I have been and still am a seeker, but I have ceased to
question stars and books; I have begun to listen to the
teaching my blood whispers to me."

Hermann Hesse *Demian*

Brianna felt herself falling. Had she fainted? At the same
time, she thought she saw her mother in the fog. She didn't
remember fog that evening. She had seen that black dog so
clearly at the end of the street. And there was light -- so
bright. Like thousands of sparkling jewels. There were
crowns and orbs and gold, inlayed with rubies and diamonds.
She tried to cover her eyes but she couldn't move her hands.
Could these be King John's treasure? Was she dreaming even
though she was awake?

Someone took her hand. It was a large, warm hand, a
female hand. "Mother?" she asked.

"No, it's not time yet." Not her mother's but her aunt
Andera's voice.

Brianna twisted her neck, she could feel the bones
cracking as she turned. Andera stood next to her, her face
solemn. "Why did you bring her here?" Her voice was angry
as she spoke to someone whom Brianna could not see.

"I had to. She had to know something." The voice
sounded hollow, and Brianna could not tell if it belonged to
a man or a woman.

"You could have spoiled the plan. She has to learn what
you never taught her."

Brianna slipped out of consciousness again, but then woke suddenly, retching. She was sitting on the step of the kitchen. An older kitchen maid held her shoulders. "You probably ate too quickly," she said. "And you not used to such rich food." She held a mug of water to Brianna's lips. "Go ahead. Drink. It's clean water from the spring. I mixed just a bit of wine in it. It will settle your stomach."

Brianna sipped and began to feel better.

"There you go," the older girl said. "You need to buck up. We leave at first light for Worcester. And all of us from the kitchen are to go, including you."

Brianna took another sip of water. She was starting to come back to herself. She remembered the black dog in the street, and the knight, and Orangino. And then she had passed out -- or had she? Because she remembered very clearly what she had seen. The gems that had sparkled in a darkened room, so bright their light hurt her eyes. And her mother was there with someone else. Was it Andera? She blinked and looked around. Across the street, on the stoop opposite, sat Orangino. He sat with his front paws tucked under his body and he faced her directly. His eyes were slits, but still glowed green, and he was staring at her intently. At least he's still here, Brianna thought. She felt stronger now and got to her feet -- no dizziness.

"I'm Maude," the kind girl who had brought the water was saying. "I don't think we actually met before."

"I'm Brianna." She straightened her shoulders. "I feel better now. Maybe you are right. I ate something that didn't agree with me."

"You'd better come help now," Maude said. "We are all to help pack up what we need for the journey to Worcester."

"I'll be right there. I just need a couple more breaths of air."

"Don't be long now," Maude warned.

Brianna crossed the street and stood in front of Orangino. "What's going on?" she whispered to the cat. He narrowed the slits of his eyes further, as if in warning. "All right. I shouldn't have asked." She felt an itching on her left ankle and remembered the dagger she had hidden. She bent to scratch the place and felt the hilt of the dagger. It was hot, nearly burning her hand. But when she touched it, the metal cooled. She breathed deeply and smelled the scents of the street -- meat frying as well as the rotting garbage of the night before. Brianna turned and ran into the hubbub of the kitchen.

Maude saved a place on the wagon next to herself for Brianna the following morning. "We will have to take turns with those who are walking," Maude said. "But I said since you were feeling poorly last night, you should ride. Otherwise, you would probably have to walk the whole way, since you are new." Brianna was grateful, but Maude seemed to be in a talkative mood, and Brianna felt like being quiet. She had not seen Orangino this morning, but she was sure he would be in Worcester when she arrived. It was cold, and Brianna was grateful for her mother's shawl, although it only made her think of the strange episode of the night before. She knew enough of the magic world to know that she had not merely passed out from eating rich food. Something had happened to pull her into the spirit world, but she had come back without learning what it was. The most frightening thing about the entire episode was something that only just now came back to Brianna. Just before she lost consciousness, or whatever happened, the older knight was standing in front of her, and he said, "I can help you." How did he know she needed help?

Brianna nearly fell out of her seat when the train of wagons came to a stop. Maude grabbed her arm. "Careful. We have to get down now and give someone else a chance to ride."

"Maude!"

"Thomas! There you are!" Maude answered, and jumped down from the wagon, almost falling against a youth a few inches taller than she was. He was lanky, his body full of right angles, with blond hair that fell into his face and a broad smile showing teeth that were just a little bit crooked. "This is my brother Thomas. He helps with the horses."

Maude took Brianna's hand as she, too, jumped down to the ground. Other servants who had been walking immediately claimed their seats. In the wagon behind, the cook was giving instructions for securing crates that had come loose. "If those plates are damaged, Lady Alice will have my head, make no mistake," she said to the frightened servants who worked to tighten the load. She cuffed a small boy who didn't move fast enough to avoid her great, strong hands.

Brianna pulled her attention back to her immediate surroundings as the wagons began to move again. Thomas smiled at Brianna. Her first impression of him was that he smiled easily. "I saw you last night, Brianna," he said. "You were with Sir Michael."

Maude looked from her brother to her friend. "You were with Sir Michael?"

"Who is Sir Michael?" Brianna asked.

Thomas's smile had faded and he looked at Maude but spoke to Brianna. "You should know. You were with him."

Realization and fear dawn simultaneously on Brianna. "The knight?" she whispered. "The knight is Sir Michael?"

"Of course he is!" laughed Thomas. "I saw you with him last night walking down the street together. I thought you were running an errand, or he was walking you home. He's old enough to be your father, with graying hair and covered with scars from battles from here to Jerusalem." He put his arm around Brianna's shoulders. "Don't worry. I can find someone young and strong for you." He laughed and his sister frowned at them.

In spite of the near accusations of bad conduct that Thomas had leveled at Brianna, she found herself enjoying his company along with his sister Maude. They told Brianna that they had worked in the household of Sir Ralph Mallory since they were small children. Their mother had died when they were young, and their father had been a groom in the stables of the same household until his death three years before. With Thomas at seventeen and Maude at fifteen, they were considered adults and performed the jobs of adults, even though both were low in the hierarchy of household servants. This trip to Worcester was a great adventure and they were in high spirits, even though the purpose of the journey was to bury King John.

That night they made a camp along the road, and the younger members of the group were in a festive mood, even though they were hushed by the adults in charge. "We'll be up before first light," the cook told her group of workers. "We must reach Worcester well ahead of the King's body and his entourage, so we can prepare food for the funeral feast."

Thomas sat on the ground next to Brianna as they ate, and she found herself enjoying his company. As much as she missed her mother and feared for the future, this companionship with people her own age was a new and pleasurable experience. When it was time to sleep, she noticed some couples sneaking off into the darkness outside the camp, but Brianna was content to lie down between Maude and Thomas. She slept deeply, and remembered no dreams, when the shouts of cook woke them. It was still dark. She felt the weight of Orangino on her feet, and sensed him stand and stretch before disappearing. She felt comforted to know he was there. A magical cat could take care of himself, but his presence calmed Brianna.

"Up! Up! Time to move!" Thomas opened his eyes and smiled at Brianna, before closing them again. He did not seem to be aware that a cat had slept next to him all night.

"Come on, Brianna," Maude said. "He always sleeps until the last second. Let's go into the bushes quickly and maybe we can get the first seats on a wagon again."

Brianna followed Maude into the bushes to a small clearing that the females were using for a privy. They hurried back, but were too late. Two other kitchen maids were already in the prize seats on the kitchen wagon. They laughed when they saw the disappointment on Maude's face. "Hope you can stay awake while you walk, Maude. If not, we'll leave you behind in the gutter."

Once again Brianna fell into step between Maude and Thomas. After being so reluctant to wake up, Thomas was full of energy as they began the second day of walking toward Worcester.

He took Brianna's hand in his and swung it back and forth playfully. "Brianna, Brianna, the lovely Brianna!"

She laughed. She could not remember anyone ever calling her lovely before. Even her mother, who loved her and made no secret of how special and precious her daughter was to her, never spoke of her beauty, and Brianna never thought about it. It wasn't important to her -- until now, when Thomas said she was lovely. Was she? She had rarely seen her own image -- only her reflection in a still pool near the village. But even the pool rippled and shimmered as she looked, and she had never seen herself clearly. Her mother told her that physical beauty was unimportant, and she believed her. But it was nice to be called lovely.

"So how did you come to join the King's household?" Thomas asked as they walked, still holding hands.

Brianna said nothing, knowing that if she admitted it was Sir Michael who had brought her there, she would hear no end of comments from Thomas. And no end of questions. But she hesitated too long.

"It was Sir Michael, wasn't it?" Thomas stopped walking and pulled her out of the line and towards him. "He's dangerous, Brianna. You don't know because you are a country girl. Stay close to me. He may leave you alone, or maybe he will forget about you." Thomas brushed his hand across her cheek. "I'll protect you, as much as it is in my power to do so."

"Back in line! Get a move on! Save that for tonight in the woods!" Everyone within earshot laughed, and Brianna felt her face redden. She was glad when the wagons began to move again.

*****

This would be their last night on the road before they reached Worcester, and the hard work of preparing feasts for all those assembled for the King's funeral began. Everyone was tired from walking. Thomas had gone ahead to help with horses at the front of the line, when the sound of horses' hooves behind them on the road caused everyone to move aside. The sound of thundering hooves always meant nobles traveling fast and on their own business. If you were in their way, you could be trampled.

Three knights on horseback passed the group. They had slowed to a trot when they reached the middle of the train, and the first in line seemed to be looking for someone. When they reached Brianna, they slowed to a walk, and Sir Michael looked into her face. Brianna looked up and then down at the ground. When she looked up again, he was still staring at her. Just as quickly he flicked his horse's reins and was off.

Worcester was wrapped in the solemn blanket of mourning for the king. But like any blanket, this one was superficial, and would be thrown off when it had served its purpose. John had not been a popular king. But the people of England still believed that the king, whoever he was, ruled by the grace of God. Good or evil, the right of the king to rule was divine. The loss of the jewels in the Wash was no longer important. Someone had them, there was no doubt. But there were more important things to be concerned about now. The jewels had done no good to John. They would do no good for the nobles.

Brianna could only hope that she would find direction for the next step of her journey after the king was buried and the court moved back to London. She was not actually part of the royal household. She had only been pulled in to work because of the king's death. The knight, whom she knew now was called Sir Michael, was nowhere to be seen. She was surprised he had not appeared at any of the feasts if he were such an important knight. But perhaps he had business elsewhere. The new king was nine years old. There was no "real king" to pander to. Brianna had decided that she would work in the kitchen until the funeral feasts were finished, and then decide where to go next. She hoped that there would be a sign by then that would give her direction.

Chapter 12

"Witches were a bit like cats. They didn't much like one another's company, but they did like to know where all the other witches were, just in case they needed them."
Terry Pratchett *A Hat Full of Sky*

Brianna woke with a burning pain in her leg. Her skirts were twisted around her, but that wasn't the cause of the pain. She rose from the pile of straw where she slept with Maude and the other kitchen maids. Once again, she longed for her comfortable bed in the cottage she and her mother shared in the village. She stepped outside into the cool air and lifted her skirt to look at her calf. An angry, red welt about two inches across marred her left calf about halfway between her knee and her ankle. What had caused it? She shook out her skirt and then she saw it. A circle just at the level of the welt was burnt to a dark brown, and just inside her hem at that point was the silver coin and the gems that she had brought from the village. She loosed the stitches in the hem and the gems nearly blinded her with their brilliance.

"Brianna, what's wrong? What are you doing out here?"

She jumped when she heard the voice, but relaxed when she realized that it was Thomas. "I ... I wasn't feeling well. I needed some air," she stumbled.

"You shouldn't be out here. It's dangerous. This is Worcester, not Newark or your village," he said.

"This is the king's court, Thomas. I'm safe enough."

He came over and put his arm around her. "I was coming to look for you, Brianna. I had a feeling you would be out

64

here," he said gently. He pulled her close until she could smell his warm breath as his lips brushed her cheek. "I want to protect you, Brianna. You are very special to me, and I don't want anything to happen to you."

"Nothing is going to happen to me," she answered, pulling back from him, but not completely extricating herself from his embrace.

"You don't know the city, Brianna. You are from a small village, and you are very young, and you are alone." He brushed a strand of her hair out of her eyes. She shivered, whether from the cold air, attraction to Thomas or something else, she wasn't sure. "You are cold. Let's go somewhere warm where we can talk."

"I need to get back." Brianna pulled out of his arms now. "Someone will miss me and report it. I could be in trouble."

"I'll take care of it, Brianna. I know people here. I'll take care of you. I promise."

"I'm not sure . . ." she began. Out of the corner of her eye, she saw Orangino sauntering down the road, his regal tail high in the air, wavering as if he were tasting the air like a snake. Thomas noticed her sideways glance and pulled away. When he saw only the cat, he grabbed her hand and pulled her into the shadows, into a tiny alcove where two sections of the building met.

"That cat. I've seen it before. But it can't be the same one. I saw it in Newark. With you." He stared at her. He started to bend to toward her and then pulled back as if repulsed. "You are a witch!" he hissed.

"What are you talking about?" Brianna answered. "Just because you see a cat that looks like another one, doesn't mean I am a witch! Have you lost your mind?"

"I know what I see," he replied, but instead of walking away, or sounding an alarm, he pinned her against the wall and kissed her. "I always wanted to kiss a witch."

"I'm not a witch!" she said, but he kissed her anyway. It felt good, but frightening. Brianna didn't know if she was frightened of being kissed or frightened because he called her a witch. She relaxed against him. What harm was there in a kiss? But when he pulled her closer and his hands began to roam, she pulled away.

"What's wrong?" he asked.

"Someone will see us," she said, knowing as she said it that it was a lame excuse.

"I doubt it," he answered. "Not at this time of night." He put his hands on her shoulders and kissed her again. She let him kiss her more deeply, enjoying the sensation that coursed through her body.

A door slammed behind them. "Thomas?"

It was his sister's voice. She stood in the kitchen door, holding a candle. "Thomas? Lady Alice wants to see you. She has a message for you to deliver." She squinted into the darkness. "Who is with you?"

"Just a witch," he laughed and kissed Brianna on the cheek. "Better get to work, my love. Or do you use magic to do your kitchen work?"

Thomas disappeared into the kitchen with his sister, and Brianna slunk into the shadows, into a tiny alcove where no one could see her. Where was Andera when she needed her?

Chapter 13

Perhaps home is not a place but simply an irrevocable
condition.

James Baldwin *Giovanni's Room*

"It won't work," Marged said, as the scrying glass
clouded. The light in the room shimmered when she spoke,
but the group of people who sat in the room were used to the
shimmering and took no notice of it. She smoothed her full
skirt, made of a deep blue wool. Her light red hair had
slipped from its bun and tendrils hung around her face. Her
fair skin was smooth but her brow was creased with worry.
"I should never have left her alone."

"You had to." Rhys emerged from the shadows to stand
before her daughter. "Neither of you would have been safe
if you had stayed. If they had executed you as a witch, you
would not be able to travel between the worlds. You go or
you stay."

"I am afraid we have put her in too much danger,"
Marged replied. She twisted her curls and then pushed them
behind her ears before standing and pacing to the fire, where
she stood watching the flames rise and fall, crackle and hiss.
"That boy, Thomas, will do her harm. I know it. He can't be
trusted."

"You are right," boomed a voice from the corner.
Jonathan, Marged's father and chief wizard, sat in the corner,
holding a sleeping child on his lap. He stretched his limbs to
ease the kinks without waking the child. "That is why

Michael, or Sir Michael as he calls himself, is there to rescue her."

"Michael!" Marged shouted. The child stirred on the man's lap, but fell back into sleep. "Michael." She repeated the name more softly, but the derision she felt was even more apparent. "Michael is nothing. He is her father in the physical sense only."

"I think you are wrong, Marged," the man said in a calm, even tone. "You never gave him a chance to be a father."

"He has no magic," she said. "He won't understand her."

"That's where you are wrong, daughter." The man handed the sleeping child to her mother, who had been kneading dough at a table in the corner, and stood. His head nearly reached the ceiling, and his lanky bones and straight, long gray hair emphasized his height. "I believe he does have magic, but he doesn't know it. And you were too young and inexperienced when you knew him to recognize it."

Marged was shocked at the vehemence in his voice. "Are you saying I . . .?"

"Why do you think Brianna's magic is so strong? It comes from both parents."

The fear that Marged had felt since the birth of her daughter thirteen years ago erupted in a strangled cry. "She is going to die!"

"No. She is not," her mother said. She gripped her daughter's arm, forcing the younger woman to look into her eyes. "But she must learn who she is."

"But you gave her some of the jewels." Marged had now turned to her sister Andera, who had walked into the room moments before and stood listening. "You have involved her in a human situation that could lead to disaster if anyone found out. Why did you do that?"

"Someone needs to serve as a link for the jewels between the worlds." Andera has lost patience with her sister, who seemed to do nothing but complain and play at magic.

"Someone who possesses strong magic, but retains ties to the mortal world, needs to hold a few of the jewels until the transition period has past. At the same time, the jewels will give her strength as she travels."

"Andera is right," Rhys added. Brianna's character is much stronger, and she is more suited to life between the worlds than you ever were. Let Michael protect her on the next part of her journey. And at some point they will both learn why they are important to each other."

Andera stood staring into the flames on the hearth, lost in thought. At last she faced her sister. "You are right about one thing. We need to get Brianna away from that Thomas boy. He's trouble, but just good-looking enough to turn a young girl's head."

"But how?" Marged asked. "If we interfere . . ."

Jonathan laughed from his spot in the corner. "What's wrong with interfering?"

"But you always told me that if we interfered, we could change the course of human history."

"My dear. You were a child then, and you didn't stay with us long enough to learn what you needed to. Did Andera interfere when she went to Brianna in the village? No. It is not interference to protect one of our own."

"So what do we do? How do we protect her without betraying her?" Marged asked.

Jonathan stood. At his full height, it was obvious that his magical powers were strong. In truth, he was one of the strongest wizards in the middle world that straddled mortals and magic. "One of you must go to Michael."

"Why don't you go?" Andera asked.

"Andera, my dear!" His eyes flashed in mock consternation. "You surely have learned by now. A man like Michael will react much more positively to a woman. I believe you should go."

Andera blushed. She did know. She had had her own share of romances with mortal and magical men. "I will go. You are right. But I think I need to go back in time, to prepare him." The firelight picked up the glints of red in her hair as she crossed the room, straightening her dress and smoothing her curls. "I'm ready."

Jonathan held out a hand to Andera. The instant their fingers touched, there was a crack as if lightening had struck, and Andera disappeared.

"I hope it goes well," her mother Rhys said. "I would so like to see my granddaughter. I've never met her, you know." She directed a glance at Marged, but said nothing more.

Chapter 14

"Everything I have to say has already crossed your mind."
"Then possibly my answer has crossed yours."

Arthur Conan Doyle, *The Memoirs of Sherlock Holmes*

The man who called himself Sir Michael did not, in truth, know who he was. His mother had been a peasant girl, that he knew. She had been beautiful, that he remembered, just barely. She had died when he was six years old. He grew up in the village where she had died, being passed from house to house, family to family. No one let him starve, but no one cared enough to give him a permanent home, either. When he was ten he was given to a knight who was leaving on Crusade with King Richard, and who was in need of a page. The knight, who was called Sir Edmund, was killed attacking Acre in the Holy Land. Young Michael attached himself to one soldier and then another; he was accustomed to being passed from hand to hand by those more powerful than he. It came to suit him as a way of life. He learned. He ate, drank and slept and then moved on. He arrived back on English soil when he was twenty. He had learned to fight, learned about women, learned to hide and be stealthy when he needed to. He spoke five languages fluently. And he had become Sir Michael. King Richard was dead by that time, and his youngest brother John was king. John Lackland, he was called, because as the youngest, his father had not seen fit to endow him with a title and land. This didn't bother the new Sir Michael. He created a past for himself from the court of King Richard and attached himself to the new king's court. The life suited him.

Then a few months ago, he was contacted by a woman who frightened him. Sir Michael always prided himself on his ability to fight his way out of any situation. He was skilled with the dagger and the sword, and if those failed him, he had extricated himself from many a tight situation with his bare hands. But this woman only looked at him with her fierce blue eyes and he trembled. It was not the trembling of the attraction of a man and woman, it was genuine fear.

He first met her in London. She was selling fine metals imported from Spain, manufactured by the Moors in that country. He had gone to purchase a dagger and wanted only the best. She showed him the blades, the differing heft and weight of hilt against blade, and he knew in the depths of his being that she could kill him if she chose. But he returned to the shop again and again. After several visits, he purchased a small dagger. It was not what he had intended to purchase. It seemed to be more of a woman's dagger -- small and light. He requested a fleur-de-lis design on the hilt, to remind himself of his time in France, but when he arrived to pick the knife up on the day they agreed upon, the hilt was decorated with Celtic swirls. He was due to leave London the next day with the King's train, so he took the knife. It wasn't what he wanted, but he felt a strange desire to own it. It would serve him in the future. Later he had second thoughts and returned to the shop in the afternoon, meaning to insist that the woman exchange it for a heavier blade, one more suited as a weapon for a knight, but he could not find the shop. He asked other shopkeepers on the same street, but none of them admitted knowing anything about the woman or her shop. The bartender in the small alehouse just two doors down the street, where Michael had stopped for a drink on more than one occasion, denied knowing the woman, her shop, or Michael.

He left the next morning on the King's progress north, deep in thought.

*****

The morning after the King's death, Michael woke with a sense that something was about to happen to change his life, something more than his position at court. He had dreamt of a beautiful woman who seemed to remind him of someone from his past, although he couldn't put his finger on who it was. Every time he tried to identify her, the thought slipped away. She was telling him something about the girl Brianna, who also seemed more than familiar in the dream. It made no sense, but the dream would not be forgotten the way dreams usually were with the morning light. He struggled to focus on his tasks for the day. The new king would need loyal knights, and he was ready to pledge his allegiance to the monarch. Michael had slept in an inn not far from the court and risen early, intending to ride to the palace and make himself known. The innkeeper was already up, tending the fire and baking bread for early risers. He greeted Michael. "Good morning, Sir! Some ale and a loaf before you go out?"

"I have no time," he answered. "But I may return later."

"Shall I hold the room for you for another night?" the innkeeper asked.

"Yes, if you would be so kind." He tossed a coin to the man and ripped off another bite of bread with his teeth.

"You will be off to serve the new king, no doubt," the innkeeper said. Although Michael had been friends with James the innkeeper for years, he could never understand how someone could be so eager for conversation this early in the morning.

"No doubt," he replied, "as we all must do."

The other man nodded knowingly. There was nothing else to be said. To admit that one was not going to serve the king, even if he were a small boy surrounded by regents, was tantamount to treason, and both men knew it. At that moment, loud voices were raised in the floor above, and the men heard the sound of boots on the stairs. Michael consciously rolled his eyes in what he hoped was a knowing manner, and bid farewell. "I see your workday has begun," he said. "And I'll be off."

Michael's horse was ready, as he had requested the night before, and he gave the young groom another coin before jumping in the saddle and riding off. Whatever the commotion was about in the inn, he wanted no part of it. His sense of foreboding was increasing, but he wanted to meet it head-on and make his own decisions. He dug his heels into the horse's sides and rode quickly through the streets, his brow creased with determination.

In the palace of Worcester, the court was preparing to leave for London. Although many knights had bedded down in the great hall of the house where the prominent members of court slept, Michael had chosen to isolate himself from that group. There was always the possibility that someone would question him too closely, and his guise as Sir Michael would be destroyed.

He handed the reins of his horse to Thomas, the young groom who seemed to be smitten with the girl Brianna. Thomas had a smirk on his face this morning, which made Michael like him even less. "She's a witch, you know," the boy said quietly.

"What did you say?" Michael glared at the boy, who stood taller, trying to appear as a man in front of the knight.

"She's a witch. That wench called Brianna. That cat is her familiar. It spies for her and helps her in her witchcraft." Thomas looked around, his wary eyes searching for other listeners in the early morning.

"Why are you telling me this?" Michael answered. He liked the boy even less now, whatever his reasons for making this dangerous announcement, because that was what it was. Even an accusation of witchcraft could put Brianna's life in danger. A conviction of witchcraft led to burning at the stake, if the tests to determine guilt or innocence did not kill her first.

"You seem to be protecting her," Thomas answered, the smirk still on his face. "I thought you ought to know who it was you were protecting, seeing as how you serve the young king."

Thomas didn't see the slap coming; all he knew was that he was suddenly on the ground, his face stinging, and his shoulder numb from where he hit the pavement.

"You little whelp." Michael dragged him to his feet. "You are as bad as a washerwoman, spreading gossip. Yes, I serve the king, and in a greater capacity than the likes of you." He brought his face close to the young groom's and hissed, "I'll see you are banned from the court and go back to tending horses at a second rate inn, where you belong." He shoved Thomas away from him.

From her dark niche beside the kitchen door, Brianna had seen and heard the entire encounter between Michael and young Thomas. She sat huddled with the cat Orangino, whose presence calmed her. But she had heard Thomas's words, even though Michael had not. As the boy slunk away she heard him whisper, "I'll get her. And I'll show him."

Brianna felt the sense of desolation she had felt before she met Thomas and his sister Maude, and thought that their companionship, especially that of Thomas, would be her salvation. She thought the king's court would offer her some measure of safety, but it seemed she was wrong. Thomas would betray her, as would his sister. And she feared Sir Michael, even though he had taken her side against Thomas. He seemed to always be nearby when she was in trouble, and she still wasn't sure if he was the cause, the catalyst or her savior.

Brianna thought of her mother, and for the first time, she believed that she was dead. There was no magic, only strange coincidences. Orangino was nothing more than an ordinary cat. True, he had protected her from danger once or twice, but now what? He seemed more interested in catching mice and grooming his already elegant orange fur than performing anything remotely magical. But maybe he wasn't supposed to do anything. Maybe it was up to her. She needed to act; he was the witness. Brianna stood and emerged from the niche into the early morning light. The sun from the east sent a glow into the dark street, and the light caught the strands of gold in her hair. Sir Michael saw her immediately.

"Brianna, what are you doing there?"

"I was hiding," she answered. "But I'm not hiding anymore."

"Come. This isn't safe." He looked around the street, but Thomas was gone, and no one else had emerged except for a couple of kitchen servants bent on their early morning errands. He held out his hand to her. "Come on. You can ride with me. I know a place where we can talk."

Brianna looked doubtfully at the huge horse Sir Michael held by its bridle, but she knew she had to take the risk. She glanced at Orangino, and Sir Michael laughed. "The cat will be fine until we get back. I have a feeling that cat knows more than we do about what's going on."

Brianna allowed Sir Michael to help her up onto the horse's back, and then he climbed up behind her. "Just hold onto his mane," he instructed. "Have you ridden before?"

"Never," she replied as she looked down at the ground so far below.

"I didn't think so." He shook the reins and the horse started to walk, and then increased its gait to a trot. "Don't worry. His name is Jupiter, but he is gentle as a lamb when he needs to be. He senses what his rider needs. He always has with me."

Brianna tightened her legs around the huge animal, loving its warmth and the feel of its powerful muscles beneath her. But she was so high above the ground! She balanced on a knife edge between fear and exhilaration. Sir Michael directed the horse out of the street and then down another, until they reached an opening that led to the river. He rode to the small inn where he had spent the night. As soon as they stopped, a young boy ran out, "Sir Michael! Are you returned for breakfast, sir? My father said you would be back." He took the horse's bridle as the knight climbed down and then helped Brianna. He did more than help her, he lifted her down. She felt a huge sense of relief when her feet touched the ground again, but also a sense of pride that she had ridden a horse, a knight's horse, even though he had been behind her on the saddle.

"Yes, we would like breakfast."

"I'll tell my father that you are here," the boy said, leading the horse away to the back of the inn.

"Come on, Brianna. These are my best friends in Worcester. We can safely talk here." He led her inside where a fire burned, and the warmth was more than physical. Brianna felt safe and at home for the first time since she had left the village. No, longer than that. Since her mother had gone.

A large man greeted them with a grin. He was large in every sense of the word. Brianna guessed that his height was almost as great as that of Jupiter the horse, and his shoulders were broad, his arms muscular. His smile was also large and lit up his face.

"Sir Michael, my boy! Happy to see you back!" he boomed as the two walked in together. He executed a broad wink that seemed to have some special meaning between the two of them, but Brianna had no idea what it was. "Is this lovely young lady your daughter? You never mentioned a wife." The two men laughed heartily at the joke and Brianna shifted her feet in embarrassment.

"A man can certainly have a daughter without having a wife, and many sons as well. But no. Brianna is not my daughter. But she is in a spot of danger and I have somehow taken on the task of protecting her. And I'm not sure how that came about." He accepted the glass of ale that James the innkeeper offered to him. He handed one to Brianna as well, and she thanked him shyly.

"How can I help?" James asked, his open face suffused with compassion and willingness to be of service.

"At the moment," Sir Michael replied after a long pull at his ale, "we would like whatever breakfast you can find for us that is edible, and a quiet place where we can talk and see if we can get to the heart of these difficulties."

"I can assist you with both of those, and willingly," James answered. His son, who was also named James but called Jamie, came in just then. "Did you take care of Sir Michael's horse? The mighty Jupiter is a very special horse."

"Yes, father. He's stabled in the usual place." The boy looked at the mugs of ale that the two visitors were enjoying.

"Good..Good. Take yourself to the kitchen and ask your mother for some bread and cheese for these two to break their fast. And then have some yourself. I have more work for you later."

The boy ran into the kitchen and they could hear him chattering to his mother. James smiled with affection at the sound of his son's voice. "He's a good boy," he said. "But I don't want him to know too much. It could be dangerous. Especially in these uncertain times." He nodded his head as if making a decision. "Follow me."

He led Sir Michael and Brianna through a door at the back of the main eating room and then up a narrow staircase. He opened a door into a small, dark room that smelled of vegetables and dried meat. "We use this for storage sometimes, but it's also useful for private conversations." A well-scrubbed wooden table with two chairs stood against the wall. James climbed onto one of the chairs and reached up to open a trapdoor in the ceiling. Immediately the room was illuminated with sunlight and fresh air, or as fresh as air could be this close to the river Thames. "Take all the time you need," he said. He pointed to the trapdoor. "It's also useful if someone needs to escape in a hurry. I'll be right back with your food."

Sir Michael nodded to Brianna that she should sit down, and the two faced each other over the bare table. "Now tell me who you are, and why Thomas the stable boy is accusing you of being a witch, and why you keep turning up in my way. And while you are at it, what is it with that damn cat of yours?"

Brianna exhaled a long breath and traced the grain of the wood in the table top with her finger. "I'm not a witch. But sometimes things happen that I don't understand."

"You are not telling me the truth, Brianna." His black eyes held hers, and she gulped.

Brianna swallowed the tears that began to well up in her chest, causing her words to emerge in a strangled whisper. "My mother told me that we were not witches. She told me never to use that word. But there are things that happen . . ."

"But you understand how and why they happen, don't you? Because they happen to your mother, too." They both were quiet when they heard footsteps on the stairs followed by a soft knock on the door.

"Breakfast," James announced. He pushed open the door and set a tray of warm bread and hard yellow cheese on the table. From his pocket he pulled a large apple, and deftly slice it in two with the knife he carried at his belt. "Only one left, I'm afraid. You will have to share." He glanced at Brianna, who was wiping the tears from her face with her hand, and then at Sir Michael, but said nothing. "Take your time," he added, then left and closed the door. They could hear his footsteps as he descended the stairs.

"He's a good man," Sir Michael said as he reached for his half apple. "None better. Now tell me. Where is your mother?"

"I don't know," Brianna replied.

"Ah," he said, as he chewed bread and cheese thoughtfully. "And you are searching for her?"

"Not really. You see, she has been gone a long time. She might be dead. But I don't think so."

"But you aren't looking for her? What are you doing then? Where did you come from?"

"I knew I had to leave the village. It's in the fens, near the Wash."

"Near the Wash," Sir Michael repeated thoughtfully. "Where King John lost his treasure."

"Yes," Brianna answered. She was nibbling the bread, but found she was not hungry. "But I don't know anything about that."

Sir Michael chuckled. "No one does. Except maybe King John himself, and he took that secret to the grave with him. He probably sold his jewels to pay his debts." He finished the last of his food and sipped his ale to wash it down. "So you left the village where you lived after your mother disappeared. And then went where?"

"I went to Newark, where the king died, and where I first saw you."

"Why did you go to Newark?"

His dark eyes seemed to bore into hers, and Brianna felt no choice but to answer with the truth. "I went with a family from the village who were willing to shelter me that far. We were friends." Her voice broke at the thought of those friends, so far away. She hoped there had been no recriminations against them for giving her safe passage out of the village, if anyone had found out. "Newark was our closest market town, and they wanted to sell a cow."

Sir Michael chuckled into his ale. "They wanted to sell a cow, and so you went along."

"I needed to go, and it would have been unsafe for me to travel alone."

"I understand. And then you found work in the kitchen of Lord . . ."

"Yes. It gave me a place to sleep, and food in my stomach until I figured out what to do next."

"And then I took you to the court of the new king, to work in their kitchen. Do you know why I did that?"

"No. Why?" She looked at him with wide eyes, hoping that his answer would provide some solution to her questions.

"I don't know either. I felt compelled to protect you. And it seems I put you in more danger, since Thomas has accused you of being a witch." He drained the last of his ale. "And it seems he is correct."

Brianna felt cold. She wrapped her arms around herself but could not stop the shivering. Witchcraft was a serious charge. The sentence was death, usually preceded by torture. And there was no fair trial. Once accused, one was as good as dead, especially a woman alone. She knew she could not escape Thomas's accusations on her own, and she was so tired of being alone. "What will you do?" She asked in a small voice.

Sir Michael studied her carefully. "I will do everything in my power to protect you from whatever dangers are threatening you."

"Why?" she whispered.

"Because I must." He pushed back his chair. "I think the first thing is to get you out of Worcester."

"Where will I go?"

"Let me think. You will be safe here. I'll be back later."

Without another word, Sir Michael disappeared down the stairs to the rooms below. She heard his voice speaking with James and his son, and shortly after she heard the clatter of horse's hooves. She sat at the table, playing with the dregs of her breakfast, and wished she had something else to drink. She did not dare go downstairs, as the inn was filling now with workmen eating their morning meal before returning to work on the docks. She missed Orangino. She missed her mother. She needed Andera's help, but where was she now? She was tired of loneliness and fear.

Chapter 15

"There is a sense in which we are all each other's consequences."

Wallace Stegner, *All the Little Live Things*

Lincoln Castle, Magic Realm

"This protection you have provided may lead her into more danger," Marged said. "He was never that smart. He wasn't even smart enough to know I was pregnant." Marged stood with her mother and her sister at the scrying water, where they watched Brianna and Michael at the inn.

"You don't give him enough credit, Marged," Rhys replied. "Or the girl. She is far more intelligent than you were at that age, or that you are now, for that matter."

"How can you say such a thing?" Marged leapt from her seat, knocking over the chair in the process.

Her mother laughed as she righted the chair with a flick of her finger and a soft glow of green light. "Then why are you here, while your daughter is left wandering, accused of being a witch by some dolt of a boy who would have made no such accusation if she had let him into her bed as he wanted?"

"What can we do?" Marged was sniffling now, and searching in her pocket for a handkerchief. Her mother handed her one from her ready supply, one of linen so white it glowed. "I raised her for thirteen years, and I didn't do that bad a job. And now you put her in the hands of a self-proclaimed knight and a cat?" The room remained silent.

"Now do you see why I left this world all those years ago?" When no one answered, Marged announced, "I'm going out."

Andera and Rhys exchanged a glance. "Out where?" asked Jonathan, who was seated in the corner listening to the women. "If you go to your daughter, you will both be in danger. You can't go back to the village. They would surely kill you. And you can't go out there." He gestured to the door that led to the outdoors and what was known as the twentieth century. "You don't know this world. The magic is gone."

Andera finally took pity on her younger sister. "Come on, Marged. He exaggerates. The magic is never gone. Only hidden." She held her hand out to her sister, pleading with her eyes for the younger woman to accept it. As soon as she had done, the two of them disappeared in a flash of light.

Marged opened her eyes to find the two of them in a dark, stone room. Reaching her hand into the air, Andera created a light. "I never could do that," Marged laughed.

Andera squelched her sister's laugh with a serious look. "That's because you don't have the focus. You don't pay attention. Your daughter does. That's why you are here, hidden in a castle at a place called Dover, and we are all trying to save your daughter's life." She slowly rotated, her arms outstretched. "You may go to any part of this castle that you can reach. If you approach the limits of your access, you will be repelled by forces you cannot see, and we will be notified. There is a place for you to sleep." She pointed to a pallet against one gray, stone wall, piled high with blankets. "And food will be provided." A table in the corner held a package wrapped in a brown cloth and tied with twine.

"You are making me a prisoner. Am I to be all alone here?" Marged gasped. "Don't I at least get a cat like Brianna?"

"It's for your own protection, Marged. I understand your worry about your daughter, and I just don't want you to do anything foolish. You will see her soon." With that, Andera disappeared.

Marged's heart ached for her daughter. She knew she had made mistakes with the girl. She had denied the strong magic that Brianna possessed. Marged had always wished she had been born mortal, but sometimes magic was just too much fun. She taught Brianna just enough to have fun, refusing to face the fact that Brianna had magical powers far beyond her mother's, and she would take it far more seriously, if Marged would allow her to.

Now she walked out of the dim room and climbed a steep stone staircase, determined to test her limits. All she wanted was to see another human face. But would her face appear human to whomever she encountered?

She had spent most of her life in either the world of magic, or the world of the village on the fens in the time of King John. Nothing in her experience had prepared her for what she saw now. Large birds flew through the air, or were they dragons? She had never seen a dragon, but she had heard of them from her family when she was growing up in a magical castle much like this one. The villagers in the fens had spoken of dragons as well, but of course no one had seen them. But the flying creatures that Marged saw now in the sky weren't dragons. She sensed something machine-like and something human in their essence. Objects fell from the flying creatures with a whistling sound and exploded in a burst of light. Fires burned where the objects landed. Marged so wanted to go out and walk on the cliffs and around the town, to escape the confinement of the castle. Tears began to seep from Marged's eyes. She was neither magic woman nor human. She was not good at being either. She seemed to slip from one to the other without warning. She hoped her daughter would be a better woman that she was.

She climbed the stairs and went back into her small, dark room, thinking she would feel better after a good cry and some sleep. Only Andera was there, seated in front of the fire where something fragrant was boiling in a pot on the hearth. Her sister smiled at her. "Come sit, Marged. I've made some tea with those flowers you brought from the village. You need to rest."

Marged sat on a smaller chair with a purple velvet cushion that she had never seen before. She was always surprised at the new objects that appeared by magic, although she shouldn't have been. She had seen it all her life. Maybe that was another sign that she wasn't meant to be a magic woman. Andera dipped out a mug of tea and handed it to her sister. Marged sipped it. Sweet, sour, spicy -- all at once. "Thank you."

"You are welcome." Andera served a mug for herself and sat in the larger chair. "Now talk to me."

Chapter 16

"We never live; we are always in the expectation of living."

Voltaire

Brianna sat in the small room above the tavern all day. She listened to the bustle of the inn below, and through the trapdoor in the roof, she could hear the bustle at the stable adjacent to the tavern. She had never lived in a place with this kind of noise and activity. The village had been quiet, and even the grand houses of the noble and the king where she had worked in the kitchen had a focused kind of noise. Once when the sun was high, and again when night began to fall, the innkeeper brought her a plate of food and a glass of ale. At noon it was another chunk of fresh bread with meat in a brown gravy, mutton, she thought. And some carrots covered in the same gravy. In the evening, it was cheese and bread again, and slices of the same meat, served cold now. After she ate, Brianna cradled her head on her arms and fell asleep at the table. She was beginning to doubt that Sir Michael would return for her, but she wasn't afraid. The innkeeper was kindness itself, and if Sir Michael did not return, she had no doubt that he would see that she was safe. The inn became hectic again in the evening, but Brianna slept and dreamed she was curled up in the corner on a pile of straw like a dog or a cat. She was warm and safe and her stomach was full.

She woke to hear a low roaring sound next to her ear, and fur tickled her nose. Then the trapdoor above her head slammed shut. She sat up straight. "I see Orangino has found you," Sir Michael said as he climbed down off the other chair. "I'm glad you've slept. We are going to ride all night."

"Ride? Where?" She stretched her shoulders and stood. "How?"

"You ask a lot of questions," he said. "Here." He handed her a bag full of food, and another that was empty.

"What is this for?" she asked, indicating the empty bag.

"More questions!" he laughed. "Orangino has to ride somewhere. Now we must go. I have safe passage for two riders. We are going south -- towards Kent."

"Kent?"

"Have you heard of it?"

"I don't think so." She rubbed her head, trying to think.

"It doesn't matter if you have or not. There is a castle there. Or if we don't make it that far, there are places where we can stay along the way. Come."

"Where is Orangino?" she asked, looking around the room. He had been in the room just a moment ago.

"Downstairs waiting for us, I would imagine."

Brianna followed Sir Michael down the stairs, but this time they avoided the crowded inn and exited into the stable yard. The innkeeper and his son stood holding two horses, Jupiter, Sir Michael's steed, and another smaller mount. Brianna stopped short. "What? I'm riding by myself?"

The men laughed. "Of course you are," Sir Michael said. "I have safe passage for two riders. That means two horses. I'll hold the reins when I can. But Belle is a gentle horse. Just hold onto her. You will get the idea soon enough."

"But my skirt!" Brianna cried.

The men looked at each other. They had completely forgotten that Brianna was wearing a skirt. "Here," the innkeeper said. "You are my son's size. Give her your breeches."

The boy blanched. "But I can't wear a skirt."

"Of course not," his father said. "Step behind that barrel and be quick now. I'll have your mother fetch your other pair, but these two have to be on their way."

The boy did as he was told and stepped behind the barrel to remove his breeches and then handed them out to his father. Brianna knew her face was as red as the dark wine drunk by the nobles, but she obediently pulled the breeches on under her skirt. They were a surprisingly good fit. She removed her skirt and stuffed it into her bag. "You make a handsome lad," Sir Michael commented. The innkeeper laughed his agreement.

"I wish I could have a look, too," the boy commented from behind the barrel. "But you will all laugh at me if I come out where I can see you."

Sobering suddenly, Sir Michael said, "We need to be on our way if we are going to reach a safe inn by first light."

"Yes. You must go," agreed the innkeeper, "and the boy and I need to get back inside before we are missed. Godspeed." He helped Brianna up into the saddle as Sir Michael mounted his own horse.

"Don't forget to get your boy some breeches before you go inside," were the last words Sir Michael said before he grabbed the reins of Brianna's horse and led her out into the street.

They rode along the river road until they reached a lone waterman who sat in his boat, ready to ferry men and goods across the Severn. "Can you carry my page and our horses, waterman?" asked Sir Michael. Brianna noticed that he sat straight in the saddle and was sure that the king's arms on his horse's bridle was turned toward the light.

"I can carry you if you have the coin to pay," the waterman answered.

Sir Michael reached inside his shirt and pulled out a single coin, indicating that there was more safely stored away.

"Very well, come on board. And here's hoping you are the first of many fares for me tonight."

"As I hope," Sir Michael replied genially. "And may God bless you." He carefully guided Brianna's horse onto the boat and into position facing the farther shore.

Brianna nodded and said a quiet "Good evening" to the boatman, hoping her voice was sufficiently deep for a page. Pages were often as young as twelve years, so she felt that she could pass for a boy whose voice had not yet deepened. But she was worried about her hair. When they left the inn, the only concern had been to find her breeches for riding. The men had forgotten about her long hair. She had quickly tucked it inside her blouse while Sir Michael negotiated their fare, but that was a poor solution. If she needed to spent much time passing as a boy, she would need to cut it. She didn't mind. In fact, it sounded like fun to go about in the freedom of a boy's short hair, and it would grow again soon enough.

Brianna snapped herself out of her reverie about her hair to notice that the boatman and Sir Michael were deep in conversation. Their voices were low, so Brianna could not understand their words. In a few moments, they had reached the south bank of the river Severn. Sir Michael handed the boatman the coins he had been promised, and gave Brianna's horse a light slap on the rump to encourage her off the boat and up to the bank. Brianna tensed, fearful that the mare would keep going, but she stopped after a few steps and waited for the other horse.

"Just follow me. The horse knows what to do. We will look more like a knight and his page if you are riding behind me, not side by side."

"Sir Michael," she whispered. "What about my hair?"

"What?" Clearly he was anxious to be off and had no time for foolish questions.

"What about my hair? I was scared to death that the boatman would see my hair and realize that I am a girl."

He gazed at her steadily for a few seconds and then smiled. "You don't know your own magic, Brianna. I see only the short brown hair of an ordinary page boy. Now let's be off." He flicked a rein and his horse moved into a canter. Brianna hesitated only a second before she copied his action, and her horse moved forward as well. The night was cool, but she could feel the warm weight of Orangino in the bag against her back and felt quite comfortable. She might learn to enjoy riding after all.

They wound their way through dark streets and soon emerged into an open road. They had encountered a few other riders, and a few folks on errands of business or pleasure on the warm spring evening, but no one took notice of a knight and page riding out of Worcester. Anyone who sought the favor of the regents of the child king would be at court. Someone riding out of the city was one less to compete for favors. And the townspeople cared little for the doings of the nobility. When they reached the open road, Sir Michael flicked the reins again and urged his horse faster. Brianna imitated his action once again, and her horse obeyed, keeping pace with the mount ahead of her. Brianna's heart beat fast, but she soon grew accustomed to the speed and began to relax once again. Strands of her hair slipped loose from their confinement in her shirt, and she relished the feel of the long strands streaming out behind her as she rode. Sir Michael had told her to trust her own magic. The boatman had not been able to see that she was a girl. But if she was safe, why did they need to ride out of Worcester in such a hurry? Once again she missed not only her mother, but the knowledge of magic she could have taught her. And what did Sir Michael know of magic? He did not seem to have magic himself, but he seemed perfectly at ease with the knowledge that she did.

They had ridden for about an hour when he slowed his mount. Brianna's did the same without her doing anything, so well-trained was she. Sir Michael moved to the side of the road and into a small woods where they would not be visible. "Few people ride at night," he said. "Better to be safe." Brianna was about to say, "But won't the magic keep us safe?" but decided to hold her tongue.

And just as Sir Michael was about to speak, they heard horses' hooves in the distance on the road from Worcester that they had just traveled. He pulled both horses deeper into the woods and signaled for Brianna to keep silent, as if she needed any warning. He stroked his mount's muzzle while his eyes studied Brianna for any sign of fear or panic. She showed none. She imitated his actions and stroked her own horse, trying to communicate a calmness that she did not feel herself. The pounding of hooves grew louder as the horse, or horses, approached their hiding place. But they thundered on past without so much as a hesitation. Brianna drew a deep breath.

Sir Michael put his finger to his lips to indicate that she should remain silent. "Maybe they weren't after us, after all," he barely whispered.

Brianna nodded, and then they both tensed when they heard a rustling sound just behind them.

"Shh. It's me. James the innkeeper." He stepped close to the two riders, leading his own mount. "I knew you would be here, Sir Michael. You are nothing if not predictable. You need to do something about that habit if you continue looking for trouble the way you do."

"What?" Sir Michael began, but James interrupted him.

"No time. I had to warn you. And I knew you usually stopped here to give your horse a breather. Someone came to the inn looking for the girl. They claim she was seen yesterday morning and then disappeared into thin air as she walked down the street, along with her cat. Her familiar, they called it." He looked at Brianna, studying her in the near darkness. He didn't believe in witches. Not really. But coming face to face with someone accused of witchcraft sometimes caused him to wonder.

"Was that who rode past on the road?" Brianna asked.

"I don't know," James answered. "I heard hooves far ahead of me, but I didn't see who it was."

"We can't go back to Worcester," Sir Michael said. "And if those are our pursuers on the road ahead, we can't continue on to Kent."

"There's a village not far from here," James said. "I think I know someone there who may shelter you for a time." He clicked softly to his horse and turned the way he had come, with Sir Michael and Brianna just behind him.

No sooner had they left the trees than they heard a shout. Someone held a torch that illuminated the scene, where two armed men sat astride horses. "There's the witch," one of them shouted.

Sir Michael and James both drew their swords and moved in front of Brianna. "Go back to the trees, Brianna," Sir Michael hissed through his teeth.

"No, I can't let you . . ."

"Go! You are no good to us here." He rode forward to the attackers where James was already engaged in fighting them off.

Brianna had no choice but to return to the relative safety of the trees. She had no sword and would not know how to use one if she did. She thought of the dagger from Toledo tucked in her boot, but she would have to be quite close to her opponent to use it. She could do nothing but watch in terror as her protectors fought against the two men who would take her captive if they could and try her for witchcraft, if they didn't kill her first. The man holding the torch that illuminated the scene was no more than a boy, Brianna noticed as he moved back and forth with the action.

Without a moment's hesitation, Brianna acted. She rode her horse straight at the youth. Her horse was too well-trained to barrel right into another human being, but Brianna rode close enough to knock the torch from the boy's hand and send it flying. In the instant that the torch illuminated the boy's face, she saw that it was Thomas, her accuser. The torch stopped in mid-air and Brianna whispered into the night, "Do damage." The torch flew on, and landed in the lap of one of the attackers, who screamed as his horse bolted in fright and pain.

The other attacker turned to see what happened to his companion, but not before he gave one last thrust of his sword into the melee. She heard a scream, followed by an oath from the mouth of Sir Michael. Had her action caused an injury or worse to the only person who could help her? The two attackers withdrew, leaving Thomas to follow after them as best he could. He gave one backward glance, a look dark with malevolence, before running after his companions into the night.

"The village." James pointed in the opposite direction from the one where the horsemen had ridden. His arm was covered in blood. Brianna rode behind them, her horse galloping, sensing the urgency of their ride. "That way." He pointed again.

They rode through some trees and soon reached a tiny cabin where a single light burned. A woman older and smaller than anyone Brianna had seen before stood at the door. "You've brought her," she said.

Sir Michael ignored her words and helped James down from his horse. He stumbled to hold him upright. Brianna slipped down from her mount and went to help. The knight looked at her sternly, but allowed her to take the injured man's other side. She was not as strong as a man, but she kept him from falling to the ground as they helped him inside.

A single straw pallet lay in a corner, the old woman's bed, and they lay the injured man on it. "He's lost too much blood," she commented, but began immediately to removed his blood-soaked clothing. "Raise his arm," she said. Sir Michael did so, and in a few moments, the bleeding had slowed to a trickle. "That's better," she said. "But we still may be too late. Let the girl hold his arm."

Brianna did as she was told while the woman and Sir Michael went to the other side of the room. They spoke too quietly for Brianna to understand their words, and soon they were back, the woman's hands filled with packets of herbs. Brianna recognized the methods of wrapping them from her mother's handiwork.

The old lady looked into Brianna's eyes. The young girl tried to pull away, but the tiny woman held her fast with her claw-like hands. "You will stay with me for a time. I can see what you need." She released one hand to point to the injured man lying on the pallet. "I will make him comfortable, but he will die. Your friend must go. He has duties of his own and he would not be safe here."

Brianna shivered. She had begun to feel safe with Sir Michael. Now she was being told that she must stay with this old woman she had just met. For how long? And was she safe here? Surely the local people knew her, and likely mistrusted her. If she was a woman living alone who knew healing, she would be named a witch, or at least suspected, just as Brianna and her mother had been. But if Sir Michael left her here, she would have no choice. And what of her own magic? She had used it against their attackers, although too late to save James the innkeeper's life, if what the old woman said was true.

Orangino rubbed against her. She had forgotten about him in the commotion. The last she had seen of him he was secure in the bag on her back. She really was not showing herself to be responsible in caring for an animal. But then Orangino did know how to take care of himself.

*****

In the castle at Lincoln, in a room outside time, three witches watched the scene in Rowena's cabin through the white flames on the hearth.

"Rowena is right," Redu said. Redu was Rhys's second cousin once removed, a powerful witch who spent most of her time in Central America in the mid-1800s. She was tall and thin, with long, straight black hair and eyes like burning coals. She specialized in spell-casting, and was often called in by other witches and wizards for her expertise. "Brianna will be safe with her for a time. Rowena knows how to cast a security spell. And between her and Orangino, they will be sure she follows the rules even if Brianna gets rebellious."

"I think she has learned enough by now to follow instructions," Andera added.

"And what of her mother?"

"Leave her at Dover. She needs to learn not to interfere. Her magic has grown weak, and she needs drastic intervention to revive it. She may lose it altogether. The daughter's strength has surpassed the mother's. I can see that soon her magic will surpass her mother's as well."

"Brianna has the potential to be a great worker of magic," Redu commented, as she prepared to return to her chosen home and century.

The three women turned their eyes away from the fire as the scene in the cabin faded. They bid each other "good night" and disappeared into points of light, which dimmed and rested.

*****

Sometime during the night, James the innkeeper died. Brianna slept in a corner, covered by a shawl belonging to Rowena, and with Orangino's warm body curled next to her. She slept soundly, exhausted by the events of the day before. She woke before it was light and heard Sir Michael and Rowena conversing quietly by the door.

"You can't go back to Worcester, Michael," the old woman said. "I have someone I can trust to send a message to his family. They can come for his body. Or he can be buried here, under the oak tree next to my man."

Brianna peeked out from under the rough blanket that covered her and Orangino. Sir Michael and the old woman still stood by the door. Brianna strained to hear their words, but closed her eyes again when Rowena glanced in her direction.

"I'll take care of the girl. I will keep her safe and I know what she needs to know. I've been in touch."

"In touch with whom?" Sir Michael asked.

"You will learn soon enough," she said. "You must go. Go west. Go to Wales if you can. Someone will be in touch."

"How will someone be in touch if they don't know where I am? And in touch about what? If you are taking care of the girl, I can just lie low until I can get back to the young King's court."

"You still don't understand, do you, Michael?" The old woman chuckled, a low pleasant sound. "You have so much to learn, more than our little girl here, I think." She glanced toward Brianna who quickly shut her eyes. "There is much in this world that you know nothing about, although the knowledge is as close as your own fingertips. Someone will find you when the time is right. I can already see where you will be in Wales. Now go! You bring more danger to all of us the longer you wait! And I have work to do."

"All right. You give me no choice." The door closed behind him and Rowena turned back to the room.

"Brianna." Her voice was conversational. She knew Brianna was awake. "Time for you to begin your day. We have much to do."

Chapter 17

"Give sorrow words; the grief that does not speak knits up
the o'er wrought heart and bids it break."

William Shakespeare, *Macbeth*

The small inn on the bank of the Severn, which had been
the home and the business of James the innkeeper since his
own father had established the inn many years before, was
the subject of a search that morning. His wife Catherine and
son Jamie stood in fear as soldiers of the king tramped up
and down the stairs of the building, finding nothing.

"Where is your husband?" they demanded.

"I don't know," Catherine answered. "He left last night
with a man I didn't know." Catherine knew that the closer
she stayed to the truth, the better off they would all be.

"An innkeeper would not abandon his inn," the leader of
the group said. He moved closer to Catherine, close enough
for her to smell his breath, stinking of ale even this early in
the morning. "Maybe your son knows something." He turned
to the boy, grabbing his hair and forcing him to stand on
tiptoe. "He is almost a man. Maybe his father told him where
he was going."

"No!" Catherine shouted. "He knows nothing."

One of the soldiers tramped noisily down the stairs and
whispered something to the captain. "All right," he
answered. He turned from Catherine. "We will be watching
the inn. And maybe we will come back for a little fun with
you and your son."

They left, but not before the captain reached a hand to touch Catherine's golden hair. Her son took a step toward them, but his mother shook her head.

When the men had gone, Catherine collapsed onto a stool by the fire. Two men who had been enjoying their breakfast in the corner walked over to her. "We've got your back, Cat. Wherever James is, you know we trust him and you. Until he returns, we are here for you."

"Thank you," she said. She closed her eyes tightly as tears welled behind them. "He's not coming back," she whispered.

Her son rubbed her shoulder, awkward for a boy of his age. "Sure he is, Ma. He has gone before like this, helping someone who had to get out of the way of the authorities."

"This is different. I know." She allowed herself another moment of tears before wiping her face with her hand. "We have work to do, my son." She smiled weakly at him. "Check those men who have come in and see they have ale, and food if that is what they want, and I'm sure it is."

They busied themselves with the morning's tasks, taking orders and carrying mugs of ale and plates of bread and cheese, and occasionally a slice of meat, to the hungry crowd. Every man who came in was known to them as a worker on the docks of the Severn, and as word had spread of James's disappearance, and the visit from the soldiers early that morning, the men assured Catherine with a word, or maybe just a look, that they were there for her. Her father had been a laborer like them, and most remembered him well, and his tragic death at the hands of King John's men just a few years before.

It was mid-morning, the sun shining through the watery clouds that covered the city, when a young man about Jamie's age entered the inn. Catherine saw him first. She didn't recognize him, but she sensed immediately the news that he carried. He looked frightened, and scanned the room for any dangers that might lurk there.

"Come. Tell me," she said, and beckoned to him to come into the kitchen with her.

"I come from Rowena, in the village of Lenning," he began, speaking as if he had committed the words to memory.

Catherine's face blanched. She glanced at her son, talking with a man in the corner, one of their regulars. It passed through her mind that this day would make her son the man that he would become. "Tell me," she said again softly. "And then I will feed you something to break your fast, for I sense you have not eaten this morning."

He felt more at ease now and stood tall, awed by the responsibility he had been given, and the woman who stood courageously before him, waiting to hear what he had to say.

"I come from Rowena in the village," he said again. "She bids me to tell you that James the innkeeper died last night in her cottage, of the wounds he received fighting soldiers who meant to capture the girl Brianna and Michael, her guardian."

Catherine covered her mouth with her hand and the tears started again, but she controlled her voice and said, "I knew. I knew something had happened. Was he at peace in his last moments?"

The boy had been told that she might ask this, and he was prepared with his answer. "Yes, ma'm. He was. With Rowena and Michael by his side."

"And what of the girl?" she asked.

"The girl lives and is with Rowena. She tried to save James, but his wounds were too severe." He stumbled over the last word, as if it were one he had been taught to say. Catherine could not resist a smile of sympathy for the boy.

"There is more," he continued. "Rowena bid me tell you that his body can be brought back to Worcester if that is your desire, or else he can be laid to rest next to her man, under the oak tree near her cottage."

"Bringing him back would be too dangerous," she said, more to herself than the boy who stood before her. "He would be pleased to rest in the ground near Rowena's man. They were always friends to us."

At that moment, young James appeared in the kitchen doorway. "Pa is dead, isn't he?"

"Yes, son. And he died bravely."

"Where?"

"In a village on the way south, at the home of a friend who took him in."

"And what of the knight and the girl?" Young Jamie bit back the emotion that threatened to overwhelm him, sensible at the same time of the fact that he must now begin to take his father's place, as keeper of the inn and protector of his mother.

The young messenger said nothing, unsure how much he should reveal. He had been running errands for Rowena long enough to know that often the less information that was known, the better it was for all concerned. "They are well," he answered finally. "Both fought bravely to save your man."

Catherine could think of no more questions, and she knew that she had no time for tears now. They would come later, when she was in her cold bed without her husband, the love of her life, to warm her and keep her safe. But she was no weak woman -- and whoever made up that fiction that women were weak, anyway? "You must be hungry after your travels from the village," she said to the boy. "Sit here in the kitchen and have some bread and cheese, and something for your thirst. Young Jamie and I have customers to attend to, but we would be pleased for you to rest as long as you like."

"Thank you, ma'm." Jamie set a plate of bread and cheese and a slice of chicken before the boy, along with a mug of small beer. His manners did not falter. He knew what his mother and father expected of him. But an anger burned inside him, anger at those who would kill his father because he was riding with a suspected witch. It was silliness. He knew plenty of witches, and there was nothing evil about them. He would find a way to avenge his father's murder, because murder was what it was. But for now he needed to keep his mother safe and help her in the inn.

Chapter 18

"Education is the kindling of a flame, not the filling of a vessel."

Socrates

Brianna stood up and stretched. She felt a sense of safety in this house, as well as anticipation. Both were feelings she had not experienced in a very long time, since before her mother had left her in the village, before the trouble started. But now she was no longer a little girl. Rowena would take care of her and keep her safe, she did not doubt that. But she knew also that the older woman was ready to teach her what she needed to know about her magical abilities. And Brianna was not only eager to learn, she knew from everything that had happened since she left the village that she needed to learn for her own survival.

"There is a privy outside," Rowena said. "And then come in and wash your face and I will comb your hair. The first thing you must learn is the importance of cleanliness."

Brianna bristled. She knew how to keep herself clean; her mother had always insisted on regular bathing, although not all the villagers saw the importance of it. But then she realized that Rowena did not know that, and she must look a mess after the ride and the fight with the soldiers in the woods. She looked down and saw blood stains on the boys trousers that she still wore, the blood of the innkeeper who died. The man's body still lay on the pallet in the corner, covered by a large cloth.

Rowena followed the girl's gaze. "We will bury him this evening. It isn't safe to dig his grave in the daylight, although most of the people in this village are no friends of the king's men. Still it is better if no one knows."

"What if they want his body brought back to Worcester?"

"They won't," Rowena answered. "They know that is too risky. And I know Catherine, his wife. It will please her to have him laid to rest here." She stopped speaking and gave Brianna a look. "Now go. Enough talk." She looked her up and down. "We have to find proper clothing for you. Blood-stained trousers will cause talk, and not the right kind of talk. I believe I have a skirt you can wear."

Brianna slipped outdoors to the small enclosure Rowena had built for relieving herself, an improvement over most peasants who simply did what they had to do a few steps from their houses. She was back inside in a moment. She rinsed her face in the bowl of water that Rowena provided for her, and dried it with a worn but soft cloth the color of dry leaves. She turned her back to pull off the torn and bloody trousers and replacing them with a dark blue skirt that made her think of the sky at midnight. Then she allowed Rowena to comb her hair. She gritted her teeth at the pain as Rowena pulled the comb through the tangles. Her hair was soft and curly and easily wound itself into tight knots. "We must do something with this," Rowena said as she put the comb down on the table. She looked around the room, searching for something to control Brianna's unruly locks. "I know." She went to the corner where the dead man lay on her pallet and opened a small wooden box. She poked with her finger at the contents removing a strip of bright blue cloth and closing the box.

"That's beautiful," Brianna said. "Where did you get such a beautiful thing?" She had asked the question before she realized its impertinence. It was none of her business.

Rowena smiled. "You are right. It is none of your business. And I believe that will be your first lesson today, to learn when to hold your tongue."

The girl lowered her head and felt the tears again. Her mother had never told her something was none of her business, even when it wasn't. And Rowena knew what she was thinking. It was a hard lesson, but one she knew she needed to learn. Her fingers reached instinctively for the edge of her sleeve, as she always did when she was upset, until she noticed that Rowena was watching her.

"I know someone else who fidgets with his sleeve like you do," the old woman said.

Brianna looked up in surprise, blinking away her tears, but Rowena said no more. She handed the strip of cloth to Brianna, who could see that it was not a mere scrap torn from a larger piece. The edges had been hemmed with careful, tiny stitches and the length embroidered with flowers of an even deeper blue. The girl stroked it, running her own fingers over the stitching. "It's beautiful," she said. "It looks fit for a lady."

Rowena took it from her and smoothed the girl's hair back from her face. "You don't need to be born in a castle to be a lady," she said. "And that is your second lesson. You are the equal to anyone, castle-born or peasant-born. A lady is a woman who stands tall and knows her role in this life. Your role in life is no lower than that of a queen, in fact, your role may be even more important." She tied the blue strip tightly, so it held Brianna's hair securely back from her face. "Much better," she said. "I can see your eyes now. And because you asked, this was made by a young girl who visited me long ago. She was your mother."

Brianna turned, nearly causing Rowena to pull her hair from its binding, since her hands were still on it. "You knew my mother?"

"Oh, yes, child. I knew her. I cared for her when she was a child. You have the look of her. But something of your father, too, of course."

Brianna turned and looked the older woman full in the face. "How did you know my mother?" she asked. "She told me she was raised in the north with her sisters. And what do you mean, the look of my father? Do you know who my father is?"

"Aye, girl. I do. But I was not sure until I had a good look at you this morning in the light." She turned from Brianna's challenging stare to stir something in a pot on the fire. "I lived in the north when I was younger. That's where I learned to make the oats that the Scots eat every morning. Down here they feed it only to horses." She ladled out two bowls full, added a spoonful of honey and thick cream, and placed one bowl in front of Brianna at the table. "Sit down, girl. Eat your breakfast. I will answer your questions as you learn magic from me. Too much knowledge at the wrong time can be dangerous. And I can see that you have your mother's impetuousness."

Brianna sat and took a spoonful of the creamy oatmeal. One taste reminded her how long it had been since she had eaten, last night in the inn in Worcester, when James the innkeeper had been alive, before they had ridden out and been attacked. She finished the bowl without another word, and looked up at Rowena. "Is there enough for me to have a second bowl?"

Rowena laughed. She had eaten only a few bites herself. "Of course. Help yourself from the pot by the fire, and the honey and cream are on the shelf."

Brianna served herself and sat down again at the table. "Thank you," she said in a soft voice.

"You are welcome," Rowena replied. "And you are very welcome in my house. It was a twist of fate, and unfortunate in the way it happened, but you were meant to be here with me. You would have faced many dangers on the road with Michael, and your small knowledge of magic could have led you to trouble."

Brianna finished her second bowl of oatmeal, and set her spoon on the table. She was about to ask another question when she was startled by two cats jumping through the window opening. One was Orangino. The other was a gray tabby a little smaller than her companion. They ignored Brianna and headed for Rowena. "I see my Shadow has taught your cat the routine here," she laughed.

"What do you mean?" asked Brianna.

"Shadow comes in every morning after breakfast to lick out my oatmeal bowl, and I always give her a little extra cream. Your cat has learned to do the same, and since we have two bowls now, it works out quite well." She placed the two bowls on the floor and the cats began to lick contently, their tails swaying in the air. "What do you call your cat?" Rowena asked.

"Orangino," Brianna answered. "But I didn't name him. That was his name when he was given to me."

"And who gave him to you?" Rowena faced Brianna and asked the question as if the answer would hold great significance.

"A woman named Andera. She . . ."

"Ah. Andera," Rowena interrupted her.

"You know her?"

"Yes, I do. Although I haven't seen her in many years. She is you mother's sister."

"Yes. She told me. But I don't understand why didn't my mother never told me about her sister?"

"I see there is much that you have not been told. And perhaps this will convince you that you have much to learn."

"But how do I know you are telling the truth?"

"First, what choice do you have?" The woman sat down across from Brianna and looked her in the eye. "You can hardly go wandering around the countryside looking for the truth. Have I given you reason not to trust me?"

"No."

"Good. There are two whom you trust who have shown their confidence in me. Do you know who they are?"

Brianna looked around. "Sir Michael and Orangino."

"Very good. Now we can begin. Do I have your trust?"

Thinking of how far she had come and the dangers she had faced since leaving the village, Brianna could only answer, "Yes."

"Can you read?" Rowena asked.

"Yes. My mother taught me. I can read English and a little French."

"Good. What about Latin?"

Brianna's eyes widened in surprise. "She never taught me any Latin. I don't know if she knew any."

"She did at one time." Rowena was silent as she laid a few packets of herbs out on the table. "You will need to learn the Latin names of the herbs we use. They are more specific than the common English names, which differ from county to county."

"I thought I was going to learn magic," Brianna said.

"And so you are. But it all fits together, you see. If you lived completely in a magical world, you would have no need for herbs, but we live in the physical world. Although some of us are fortunate enough to be connected to the magical world, our work must be done here."

"And my mother? Where is her work? Is she in this world or the magical world?"

Before Rowena could answer, there was the sound of a horse in the front yard. The old woman rose calmly and looked out into the bright morning. After learning who her visitor was, she opened the door. The young boy who had gone to Worcester to take the news of James the innkeeper's death to his family had returned. He huffed and puffed as he came in the door. He had obviously ridden hard.

"If you exhausted that horse as much as you have exhausted yourself, I think you had better see to him before you tell your news," Rowena said.

"I'll take care of it," Brianna offered.

Rowena gave her a look, and said, "Very well. Go."

Brianna slipped out, happy to do something constructive to show that she was capable and willing to help out. She had learned to care for horses in her few visits to the stables with Thomas. The thought of him still filled her with a strange mixture of attraction and fear, but she thrust those thoughts away and found an old cloth hanging outside the door to rub down the animal. "There now," she crooned. "You will feel much better now. I'll get you some water." The horse nickered softly, seeming to appreciate her attention.

When the horse had been rubbed down and provided with water and oats, Brianna went back to the cottage. She paused for a moment on the stoop, listening to the voices inside, but they were too soft for her to distinguish the words.

"Come in, Brianna," Rowena called. "You are welcome to hear everything that young Ralph has to say. You don't need to hang about on the stoop."

Brianna stepped inside, the dim interior blinding her eyes for a moment.

"The family agree that James will be buried here, under the tree next to my man who has been dead these last ten years." Rowena made the statement with a lack of emotion. "Young Ralph and his father will come tonight after dark to help us dig the grave and lay the man to rest. Better it's done quietly. The villagers don't need to know."

"Isn't it possible someone will see the grave?"

Young Ralph looked from Rowena to the girl. He would never dare to question Rowena in that way.

"Maybe they will. Maybe they won't. I think they won't." Her words contained a finality that told them as clearly as if she had spoken the words that that was the end of the subject. Brianna said no more. She stood, feeling the blush of embarrassment creep up her neck. Once again she had questioned something that was not for her to know.

"You go on home, Ralph," Rowena said, standing from the table. "Your mother and father will be wondering where you are, and I am sure they have chores for you to do."

Ralph nodded and was out the door without a glance for Brianna, who continued to stand.

"Come and sit down," Rowena told her. "Burying a man is a hard thing. We take a closer look at death than any of us want to, especially when the man has died violently before his time. This will be your first lesson in the connections of the two worlds. I believe you have the strength to pass the test."

Chapter 19

"Time is an illusion."

Albert Einstein

Dover Castle, 1940

Marged wanted nothing more than to escape Dover Castle, but she was not only trapped in the castle by magical bonds, she was trapped in the future, or the future relative to the time of King John. The air was fraught with fear and tension as the loud, metallic birds flew overhead. Marged was meant to spend her time in the oldest section of the castle, the section that had been built in the time of William the Conqueror, one hundred and fifty years before her time. But she knew that war raged outside, a more vicious and frightening war than anything she had ever known. It was her punishment for running away and raising her daughter without the magical education that she deserved. And it had turned out that Brianna had more magic, and more awareness of how to use it, than she had ever imagined. Had Brianna's father been magic after all? She paced the corridor, glancing out occasionally when the sounds from the sky were especially deafening. She wondered where they were going. Across to France, she guessed. One night one of the metal birds had returned with fire bursting from its belly. She had thought it was a dragon, but the bird crashed to the ground in a ball of flame. She felt the death of the man inside the fiery bird and shivered. Her magical guardians could not have found a more effective punishment than the one they had devised for her.

Marged decided to explore the castle, to go as far as she could and then see if she could test the magical barriers holding her within its walls. Her slippers made no sound as she walked down the corridor to where it turned before continuing on to the end where she reached a set of stone steps rising to ground level. She felt the air snap as she broke the spell that was meant to confine her to the innermost part of the castle. Her father, and everyone else, would know immediately, but she didn't care. Marged breathed in the night air and flung out her arms as if to embrace to stars that dotted the moonless sky. She wondered why there were no more lights except for the stars and the metal birds that passed overhead. Even in her old world, cottages were lit by candles, and she could sense that there were people about.

Out of the corner of her eye she caught a glimmer of light. She glided soundlessly toward the glow. She did not believe that anyone would be able to see her, since she was in a different realm of existence from theirs, but she was not sure if they would be able to sense her presence in any way. It probably depended on their ability to feel magic. Would people believe in magic in the future? How far in the future had she been sent?

At last she was close enough to see two young men standing close together just inside a doorway. They held glowing sticks of fire in their hands, and occasionally held them to their lips, which caused the ends of the sticks to glow brighter. After a few minutes, they extinguished the sticks and stepped out into the dark night. A breeze blew her skirt and she lowered her hands to still its movement.

"What's that?" asked one of the men.

"What's what?"

"I thought I saw something."

"A plane?" He scanned the starlit sky.

"No. Over there." He pointed into the gloom.

"You're imagining things," his companion laughed. "Just because this castle is almost a thousand years old doesn't mean there are ghosts here."

"And why wouldn't there be?"

"You're kidding me, right?" He peered into the darkness before adjusting the rifle on his shoulder. "Because there is no such thing as ghosts. That's why."

"I dunno, Tom. There's just something creepy about this place. I don't mind it in the daytime, or inside the bunker where everyone is so busy with the radios and all, but out here at night. There's more than meets the eye. That's what my granny always said."

"Well, go on back in then if that will make you feel better. I need a few more gulps of fresh air before I go back underground. Now that's what gives me the willies, being all closed in below ground and no windows, just ventilation shafts."

Alone, the young soldier stared into the night, wondering if his friend had really seen something. He told him he didn't believe in ghosts and such things, but he had heard stories growing up. The churchyard in their village was hundreds of years old, and he and his buddies had dared each other to go in there at night, but he never did. He didn't know if anyone else had.

He was about to turn and go back inside when he thought he saw a woman's skirt sway in the breeze, except there wasn't any breeze. He rubbed his eyes and looked again. "Hello?" He wished he hadn't told George to go back inside. "You aren't supposed to be here. This is military property."

He heard a swish and saw -- he knew he saw -- a woman pass by him. She was not very tall, with reddish blonde hair flowing down her back. Her dress was gray or blue or green, a pale shade, and old-fashioned. If he hadn't known better, he would have thought she was from the Middle Ages, when this castle had been built. He called to her again, or at least he thought he did. But she was gone.

Marged went back inside the inner castle to the rooms she was assigned. She knew she would be in trouble for venturing so close to the soldiers. Her father had used a simple spell that she easily broke. He probably expected her to try. But what if he sent her someplace else, where there was no chance she could contact anyone in the future or the past? But that was impossible. There had been people in England for millennia, and there would be for many centuries to come, of that she was sure. And it was worth it to see the look on that soldier's face, after he told his companion he had seen nothing. Yes, it was all worth it. If only she had had the opportunity to show her daughter Brianna how much fun magic could be. But she feared her daughter would be taught to take her powers much too seriously.

Chapter 20

"It's much easier to not know things sometimes. Things change and friends leave. And life doesn't stop for anybody."

Stephen Chbosky, *The Perks of Being a Wallflower*

With the help of young Ralph and his father, it had not been difficult to dig the grave for James the innkeeper. As they worked in the moonlit night, Rowena calmed the two young people, Jeffrey and Brianna, with stories of her youth. She told them of her marriage to the man who lay beneath the ground just next to the new grave. She had buried two young children as well, and a son lay buried in a distant land where he had gone to fight with King Richard, King John's older brother. "You must not fear death," she told the young people. "Or being around the dead. Their spirits live on, just as the priest tells us in his church, although I suspect it is not quite as he describes with his fires of hell as punishment and choirs of angels to serenade you if you follow the rules." She looked at Brianna, and the girl could see the woman's eyes glowing in the near dark. Brianna didn't know what to believe. Her mother had not sent her to church. She had simply told her that what she would hear there was nonsense and would only confuse her. And from the little she heard from her playmates who attended the small village church, she believed her mother was right. But her mother never taught her what to believe. Brianna had come to believe that her mother didn't know as much as she pretended to, and she might now have a chance to learn from Rowena.

It was three hours past sunset when the grave was ready. "Let's go inside the cottage and prepare ourselves," Rowena said to her companions.

"Prepare ourselves?" Brianna asked. "What do we need to prepare?"

Rowena smiled tolerantly, but Ralph had done this before. "We have to . . .," he began. He glanced at his father who frowned.

"Hush," Rowena said. "Your voice is too loud for the dark of night. This village knows me, but they trust me to keep my activities quiet. Come inside and we will talk."

She led them back into her cottage and without a sound locked the door behind her. She stirred the embers of the fire until a soft glow infused the room. Then she sprinkled some herbs from a clay jar on the mantle onto the fire. The flames sparked and crackled for a few moments, and tiny points of light shot from the fire into the air. A fragrance spread throughout the room that made Brianna think of home. It was a scent of sadness and love, and she thought her heart would break, although she didn't know why. She started when Rowena slipped her arm around her waist. "Come, child," she said. "The grief is not for you. You must learn to control what you feel."

Rowena pulled a cauldron of warm water away from the hearth where it had been waiting for them. She added a few drops of a liquid from a vial and stirred the mixture with a wooden spoon. "We will wash." She handed small squares of cloth to Ralph, his father, and to Brianna, and took one for herself. Brianna watched the others, then followed their example, dipping the cloth into the water and wringing it out, and then washing her face, arms and hands. They repeated the washing three times.

The body of James the innkeeper had been washed and prepared for burial early in the day. Brianna had not been part of that. He was wrapped in a winding cloth that had once been white, but although it was not pristine, it covered him securely. Brianna wondered how they would move the heavy body to its resting place. It was not a long distance, but it would be an awkward task. As she wondered, there was a soft knock on the door. Brianna jumped in fear, but Rowena calmly lifted the bar to admit two men. No one spoke; they nodded at each other. The two men, who wore dark clothing with brimmed hats pulled down over their faces so their features were invisible, approached the pallet where the body lay. They bowed their heads with respect for a moment before moving to each end and lifting the body. Ralph and his father moved to each side to assist in lifting the burden. Rowena nodded to Brianna, and the six of them, with the body of James the innkeeper, walked on silent feet out the door to the gravesite.

Ralph's father helped the other two men lay James's body in the grave and quietly replaced the earth on top of it. The shovels made a soft swooshing sound each time a mound of earth was moved. They smoothed the dirt and then Rowena produced a basket of dried leaves which she strewed over the grave. The leaves gave off a pungent scent and Brianna inhaled deeply. Rowena heard the girl's breath and took her hand, placing it into the basket and whispering, "Scatter the leaves. It's a connection between the living and the dead." Brianna did as she was told, and felt a sense of peace pervade her body. *Everything is connected*, she thought.

"Body below. Spirit on high," Rowena whispered into the night.

"For eternity," breathed the men and the boy.

"For eternity," repeated Brianna. Her eyes had grown accustomed to the dark, and she just was able to see two of the men slip off into the night. Then Ralph was gone, silent as well. The last man seemed to fade into the darkness. Rowena took Brianna's hand again and led the girl back to the cottage. She dipped out a cup of a warm infusion that simmered over the banked fire.

"Drink," Rowena whispered. "It will give you strength and help you sleep." Rowena poured herself a cup and the two drank.

Brianna found the drink soothing. It was slightly tart but with a sweetness that lingered after she swallowed. Rowena lay her hand on Brianna's cheek. "We'll talk in the morning. Now we must sleep." The older woman went to her bed, where the body of James the innkeeper had lain just a short while before. Brianna went to her own spot where she wrapped herself up in the blanket Rowena had given her. As she drifted off to sleep, she felt the warm body of Orangino as he settled himself next to her, purring. Where had he been all evening? Probably hunting with Rowena's cat Shadow. Tonight's business had nothing to do with cats.

Chapter 21

"You don't need to know what you're escaping from to become a fugitive."

Bella Pollen, *Midnight Cactus*

Michael rode his horse hard across England toward Wales. He would find safety there. Wales was not yet subjugated to English law, although it was not for lack of trying on the part of the English. But the Welsh stuck to the old ways and fought hard. They knew their hills and valleys well and were determined to protect them from whom they thought of as invaders. It has always been so, when one people seek to dominate another. He spent a night in a woods of oak trees, and although he lay down on the ground and stretched out his legs, he slept only fitfully, fearful that he would be discovered. But the next night, he was near the Marches, the land that bordered Wales, and felt more relaxed. He woke in the early morning to the cold nose of a dog sniffing his head. When he jumped to his feet, he was met by childish laughter. A girl of no more than ten, with black hair and sapphire blue eyes, stood a few yards away.

"Mama says you are to come and break the fast with us," she said in a clear bell-like voice. "And bring your horse up to be fed as well."

Since he was discovered, Michael saw no alternative but to accompany the girl to the small cottage that was just visible through the trees. He must have been extremely tired last night, or he would never have camped so close to a house. But it was doubtful they would turn him in to the English authorities, not in this part of the country. He untied his horse from the tree where he had spent the night and followed the girl to the cottage. She pointed to a trough of water for his horse, and another where he could wash the sleep from his face. "My brother will feed your horse," she said. She fearlessly approached the huge black stallion and touched his flank with her hand. He turned his head to her and nickered, allowing her to caress his muzzle.

"He likes you," Michael said.

"Yes," was her only answer, as if she expected nothing less.

In the cottage, a man and a boy sat at the table, eating from wooden bowls and washing their meal down with mugs of ale. Michael was suddenly thirsty. He had ridden so hard yesterday, he had barely stopped for food or drink. At midday he had risked buying a meat pie in a small village, but had he drunk anything? He couldn't remember.

The man and boy looked up and nodded at him without speaking. They seemed to accept his presence as expected. The woman turned from the fire and smiled. She possessed the same dark hair and blue eyes as her daughter. "It's only porridge," she said. "But it will keep body and soul together awhile longer. And would you take a mug of our small beer? I make it myself."

"I would indeed," Michael answered. He could feel the saliva in his mouth. He thanked her and sat to drink. He could have drained the mug in one long pull, but he controlled himself. He did not want to appear greedy. The woman set the bowl in front of him, and he ate more quickly than he intended. When he looked up, both the man and the woman were smiling at him. The boy had disappeared, presumably to go and feed Michael's horse.

"Would you like another bowl of porridge?" the woman asked, her voice kindness itself.

"I would, but only if you can spare it." Michael's stomach grumbled to punctuate his answer.

She refilled his bowl and set it before him. "There is plenty of ale as well. Drink. I'll pour you another mug."

Michael began to eat again and thought. These people seemed perfectly comfortable with welcoming a stranger into their small home. They evidently saw no danger in him. And why would they? He was alone. This was their country.

"You had best wait until nightfall before traveling again." These were the first words the man had spoken. "We are close to the border with Wales here, but still on English ground."

"How do you know I am traveling to Wales?" The question was out before Michael could stop himself.

The man smiled, pushing his black hair back from his forehead. "Why else would you be sleeping rough? And no food and drink in you for most of yesterday, I would guess." His eyes met his wife's in some unspoken communication, born of long association and common thoughts.

"Rowena told us we might see you," she said softly.

"Rowena? But how . . . .?" It had only been two days since he left Rowena's cottage and young Brianna. How could Rowena send word that quickly? Unless . . . "You and Rowena . . ."

"Hush," the woman said. "The less you know of these things right now, the better. Isn't that right, George?" She turned to her husband.

"Oh yes," he said. "Especially when it is woman to woman."

"When you reach Wales and safety, there are many things that you will learn," the woman continued.

"That's what Rowena said." Michael's statement came out lame and weak, but he was tired and confused. His head dropped to his chest.

"You gave him too much," the man commented.

"He will be all right. He needs to rest. And the fewer questions he asks, the better."

The couple helped Michael out of the chair and to a pallet made up in the corner near the fire. As soon as he lay down, he was soundly asleep. The man pulled off Michael's boots while his wife covered him with a thin blanket. Their eyes met again in silent collusion, before they left him to go about their day's work.

He woke suddenly, and could feel that he had slept several hours. The sun was high, maybe even past its zenith, and although the cottage seemed empty, he could hear voices just outside. Michael sat up, stretching his limbs. He heard the laughter of children and the baaing of sheep; then the low voice of a man giving instructions. It seemed a safe, idyllic haven, just on the edge of the chaotic English world. As he became more wakeful, his memories of the day before returned with more clarity. This family had been expecting him, and they knew he was coming from the witch Rowena. How had they known that, if they did not have some powers of witchcraft themselves? Nevertheless, he felt he needed to move on, deep into Wales. He was not that important, and the English authorities had other fish to fry these days with the new young king on the throne. He was just a minor knight and had committed no crime. The one who was in real danger was Brianna, if she were found and the accusation of witchcraft held up.

A shadow darkened the doorway of the cottage. "So you are awake?" The man spoke English, but with a Welsh accent, which Michael had not noticed earlier. "My name is Dewi. I don't think I introduced myself earlier. There is some bread here for you, and some of our fresh cheese."

"I thank you," Michael said. "A moment?" He gestured toward the outside with his head.

Michael went out to the privy, pausing to splash water on his face at the trough. He returned to find Dewi seated at the rough wooden table. Michael joined him and removed a cloth from the plate of food left for him.

"You can't stay here, you know," Dewi said.

"I know," Michael replied around his mouthful of food. He was secretly relieved to hear the farmer admit that although welcome, the visitor could not stay, for his own safety and theirs.

"It's not a matter of safety," Dewi continued. "We could keep you safe, but this is not your destination. The Brecon Beacons. I believe you will find what you're are seeking there. I can give you directions and something that will allow you safe passage through the farms and villages. It isn't that far, but Welsh hills and valleys are confusing, and Welsh people tend to stick to their own. We don't take to outsiders, unless they are known to us, and no friend to the English. Although a knight, I believe you are no friend to the English." He looked at Michael inquiringly.

Michael had finished his food and drunk the glass of ale that accompanied it. He wondered how Dewi knew so much about him, but referred to him as a knight. "I am no knight," he said.

"Ah, but you ride like one, and walk like one, and carry the King's emblem on your horse's bridle. And you are English. To all appearances, you are an English knight." He laughed then at the look of consternation on Michael's face. "It's all right. You will pass safely. No English knight would be riding alone into the Welsh hills unless he were running away from the English."

"I speak no Welsh," Michael said.

Dewi rubbed his whiskered chin. "Now that may be a problem. The farther you go into the hills, the less English you will hear, and the less the hill dwellers will want to hear the English spoken." He was thoughtful for a moment, listening to the voices of his family outdoors. "I think I will send my son with you. He has been longing for adventure, and this may be what he needs before he settles down. He may even find a wife to bring back. He's old enough." The man stood and strode to the door in two long steps.

"Mory! Come!"

A tall lad of about seventeen ran to the door. "Yes, da?" Dewi seated himself again and looked fondly at his son, who resembled him in looks, although he was taller and still retained the slim agility of youth. "Pack a traveling bag. You are going to go with Michael here to the Brecon Beacons."

"I am?" The boy's eyes widened.

"Yes. You have been pestering me for an adventure, for something different from this old farm. This will get the wanderlust out of your young blood. At least I hope it will. Michael speaks no Welsh, so you can translate for him. You will both be safe enough. There are no man-made dangers along the way. And the natural dangers we can't avoid, either at home or on the road."

"How will we know where to go?" Mory asked. "I've only been out of our valley once, and that was just to Tintern."

"You are going to the Brecon Beacons," his father repeated. "I think the near slope mountain peak is where Michael is bound. But you don't need to travel that far. It should take you a seven day or so to reach the base of the mountain. Michael will know then where he is to go. It should take you the same amount of time to return. If you want another seven day, take it. There may be young women you can meet. You may find a wife. But I will expect you by All Saints Day. It will begin to be cold by then."

Michael felt that his journey was being taken out of his hands. How did these people know where he was supposed to go? But he had ridden toward Wales, partly became Rowena had told him to. He was beginning to feel that he was not making his own choices or decisions. Unseen forces were guiding his life, and it had been this way ever since he met that girl Brianna. She was a witch, of that there was no doubt. But she had done nothing herself. There were forces around her that swept them both along, thwarting his resistance. His intention to return to the king's court and find a place to advance himself had fallen to the wayside. He set out with the boy, deep into the Welsh countryside, and instead of feeling afraid in this strange country, he began to feel at peace. It was not merely a sense of safety as his left the land of the English behind. He felt a sense of serenity. It was a strange sensation. He could not remember a time in his life when he felt like this. His memory of his parents and his childhood was too dim. He must have been a happy child because he remembered the love of his father and mother. He had felt a certain joy during relationships with women in his life, but there had always been a tension, a sense that the happiness would not last. Now he felt more than happy; he felt calm. He looked around at the sky and the rise of mountains in the distance. The leaves on the trees were turning to gold, and birds called to each other. The world was beautiful.

Chapter 22

"The most intriguing people you will encounter in this life are the people who had insights about you, that you didn't know about yourself."

Shannon L. Adler

Brianna followed Rowena dutifully through the forest, gathering the last of the herbs on the crisp fall day. The air smelled crisp, too, with an earthiness that reminded her of her forays with her mother on this same errand when she was a child. Her memory of herbs and their purposes was returning to her, and she basked in Rowena's praise. She quizzed the girl as they walked along, and every day trusted her more and more with the tasks of hanging the plants to dry in the rafters of the cabin, and to prepare distillations that could be used to treat illnesses of the villagers over the winter. "They will be coming to me with the usual coughs and colds and fevers. I will keep the proper concoctions ready." She turned to Brianna and moved closer to her so the girl was forced to stop. "I treat them with my medicines, which they know come from the plants that grow in the woods. They depend on me and protect me. This is not magic."

"But you do magic, too, don't you?" Brianna's voice was soft, matching Rowena's own.

The old woman smiled. "What is magic? Is it what you believe? Is it the power inside you from the moment you were born?"

Brianna had never thought about it. "Orangino is magic." She thought of how the cat had protected her in the city. He was now enjoying a sleep in the sunshine with Rowena's cat. There was safety enough here that he didn't feel the need to follow Brianna everywhere she went.

Rowena laid her wrinkled hand on Brianna's arm. "Yes. Orangino certainly is magic. But he has no more magic than you have. Learn from your cat, Brianna. Orangino has a strong sense of himself, as all cats do. Find your sense of self."

Brianna bristled slightly. "I know who I am."

Rowena's touch remained constant, and the tone of her voice did not change. "Not yet you don't. But you will learn. You have no choice."

"I always have a choice. That is what my mother taught me."

"Your mother made many mistakes. Part of my task with you is to correct the errors of your mother. Perhaps it's time to show you how strong your magic is, and why you must listen and learn."

In the silence that followed her words, the old woman and the young girl both heard the crack of a branch. Too loud and forceful for a small animal to make, it could only be another human being. They may not have heard the two woman speaking quietly, or they may be following them for their own purposes. Rowena always emphasized how safe they were here in the village in Worcestershire, but no one was completely safe from the evil that seemed to lurk around the corner for anyone who dared to lead a different life from most, especially if that person was a woman.

Rowena's eyes flashed and her back stiffened, telling Brianna that the woman had heard the crack and was aware of possible danger. But she smiled at Brianna and spoke clearly, loud enough for anyone in the vicinity to hear. "It's time we were getting back to the cottage. It will be a night's work to prepare these herbs. Here. You carry this basket on back for me, and I will gather just a few more of the mallow that I see just beyond that log." But she did not hand the basket to Brianna or move toward the fallen log. Instead she silently took Brianna's hand and led her to another path that branched out from the one they had taken from the cottage.

Brianna looked questioningly at Rowena, but the woman's eyes were on the forest, alert for any movement. She led Brianna down the path for about twenty yards and then stopped. Another crack broke the silence. Whoever it was, he or she was making little effort to be quiet, or else they were just careless. Now Rowena did hand the heavy basket of plants to Brianna, and held her finger to her lips for silence. Brianna felt for the dagger she always carried, hidden in her skirt pocket now. "Come out here so we can see your face," Rowena called. "Only a coward shadows two women in the forest. What are you afraid of?"

Two boys about Brianna's age emerged from the trees, each with sling shot in his hand.

"I see. You are after birds. And decided to stalk us as well," Rowena said.

"No. I mean yes. We are hunting blackbirds. We mean no harm." The boy who spoke was tall and thin, with lanky yellow hair that fell into his eyes.

"Who are you?" Rowena asked. "I haven't seen either of you around here before, and I know everyone in the village."

"We belong to the estate of Lord Elman." The second boy was shorter than his companion, with dark hair and a tendency to chubbiness. "He has been given possession of the estate just over to the river Lees, and we have permission to hunt blackbirds here." His voice and the set of his shoulders showed defiance.

"I see." Brianna's gaze switched back and forth between her mentor and the boys. Whether they were sent to spy on Rowena, and maybe on Brianna as well, or were doing as they claimed and simply hunting blackbirds, was impossible to tell. But their presence, and the presence of a new lord at the nearby estate, boded more trouble than good news. Rowena straightened her back. "My young friend here and I were about to return to our cottage for some refreshment. The sun is warm today and we have been working for some time gathering herbs to dry for the winter. Would you like to join us?"

The two boys looked at each other. "I think we should probably get back," the tall, blond one said. The other looked a shade disappointed, and Rowena took advantage of his obvious love of food. "Too bad, but I understand. You don't want to get in trouble with your master. I had made some cakes with a bit of honey, and apples as well, but . . . another time."

She turned to resume her walk down the path, with Brianna following her.

"I think we have a few minutes," the short, chubby one announced.

Rowena turned around and saw the hunger in his eyes. He was not a greedy boy, just one who liked to satisfy his appetites. She could use that quality in him to her advantage. "Come then." She resumed her walk, followed by Brianna, and the two boys bringing up the rear. That the taller boy had follow so readily, and without an argument, was significant, Brianna thought. None of them spoke until they reached cottage at the edge of the village. Then the taller boy spoke up. "What village is this?"

"It's the village of Malvern," Rowena answered.

"I think we have come quite far from Lord Elson's estate." The two boys looked around nervously.

"Not so far. You will easily be back by nightfall."

She led them into the cottage and served the cake and sliced apples on wooden plates that had been sanded and polished to a silky smoothness. "I don't have guests often.

But I am pleased that you could join us." Rowena herself stood, and ate only a minute piece of the cake. Brianna sat self-consciously at the table with the boys. She did not know how she should act with them. They could mean trouble, or they could be friends, and she had no idea which way the tide would turn.

When they had finished, Rowena announced suddenly, "Brianna. Walk the boys back through the village to the other side of the blacksmith's shop. The road there will lead them back to the estate."

Brianna gave the older woman a startled look, but Rowena only nodded. Was this part of learning about her own magic? The boys thanked their hostess politely, and she noticed that both had cleaned their plates until they almost shone. Orangino stood and stretched in his spot outside the door, and Brianna saw that the cat was following them at a discreet distance.

The two boys chatted happily as they walked with Brianna back through the village. They either didn't notice, or did not care that an orange cat followed them, or that the girl with them kept one hand tucked in her pocket where she held the hilt of a magical knife. Several villagers greeted Brianna, who was now accepted as an orphaned relative of Rowena. They looked curiously at the boys but said nothing. Brianna said goodbye to them just past the blacksmith shop, where they invited her to visit them sometime at the manor. Brianna promised she would if Rowena would allow her to come, but she knew she would never go. She was too old to play at hide and seek and climbing trees, even though the boys were nice enough, and only a couple of years younger than she was.

When she returned to Rowena's cottage, the older woman was standing in the doorway waiting. Her face was anxious and Brianna's first thought was that there was news from the city of Worcester, that she had been found and must return to be tried as a witch. But no. Then there would be soldiers about.

"There is news," Rowena stated, as soon as Brianna was close enough to hear. "Thank God you have returned."

"What has happened?"

Rowena studied the girl, as if judging her mettle. At last she spoke. "I will die soon. Not tomorrow, but soon."

Of all the thoughts that had flittered through Brianna's mind as she waited to hear what had troubled Rowena, she had not thought of something so personal. And she immediately felt guilty for thinking of possible events that would affect her -- Brianna. She had not thought of a tragedy for Rowena.

"Oh, no. But surely. . ."

"Surely what?" Rowena answered rather more sharply than Brianna expected. "Surely with my herbs and magic I can cure myself? It doesn't always work that way, my girl."

"I'm sorry. I only meant . . ."

"It's all right," Rowena touched the girl's cheek with fingers stained green from working with herbs. "I should have softened the news for you. I forget that you are not used to magical ways, nor are you of the religion of the townspeople. Come inside and we will talk."

Brianna helped Rowena prepare their evening meal, and as they worked Rowena told the young girl that she had long suffered from headaches and blurred vision, and in the past weeks both had worsened. She had believed for some time that she might have a growth in her brain, and she believed that was what was causing her problems. "It's time. I have lived a long life, maybe three times as long as most villagers. I have no regrets and no fears. Remember -- there are other worlds besides this one."

"But you said that if a person dies, we can't see them. It is only if a person goes to the magic world that we can pass back and forth between worlds. Like my mother and Andera.

132

Why can't you just go to the magic world?" Brianna realized that there were tears in her eyes. She had known Rowena such a short time, but she had grown close to her. She couldn't bear to lose another person that she cared about. But there I go again, she thought. Thinking only of myself. I must think of Rowena. But even as she thought it, she felt panic rising inside. What will I do? I will be all alone again.

Rowena gently took the bowl of greens that Brianna had just removed from the pot and set them on the wooden table. "It's not healthy to eat tears. And I'm afraid you are crying into our supper. Come sit and we will talk about what we will do."

As they ate, and Brianna struggled to control her tears, they talked of what they would do in the weeks or months that remained of Rowena's life. "I will teach you as much as I can of the old ways," Rowena said. "I have many good days ahead of me, if the Divine is willing." She reached out and lifted the hem of Brianna's skirt. "And you have been given stones from the old king's treasure. That is more than valuable in the currency of men; it is a sign of your worth. But as any possession or quality, it has a dark side. It could put you in terrible danger."

Brianna looked at the older woman in shock. How had she known about the gems? But on second thought, if she had known, why had she waited until now to say something?

"You knew," Brianna said.

"Of course," Rowena answered. "The gems were given to you by magic. Surely you know that. Those gems in the hem of your skirt are as visible to my eyes as it would be on a chain around your neck."

"Why do I have them?" Brianna had forgotten the food that was cooling in front of her. "I thought it had something to do with my mother."

"It does, after a fashion." Rowena took up her spoon. "But eat, dear. We will talk later. I need my strength, and you need yours, too, to face what is to come."

Brianna was in no mood for food, which even with Rowena's careful seasoning tasted like sawdust in the girl's mouth. Why did everyone she began to love just -- disappear? But she did as she was told and finished her meal.

Chapter 23

"Funny how 'question' contains the word 'quest' inside it, as though any small question asked is a journey through briars."

Catherynne M. Valente, *Under in the Mere*

Magic Realm

"Rowena will teach her well in the months before she dies." Jonathan raised his head from the scrying bowl, a crystal bowl filled with pure water which enabled him to see Rowena and Brianna in the cottage. "It may be better this way. The girl has a tendency to become dependent on others. She needs to develop strength and independence."

"She is young," Andera said.

"She is young," he repeated, "but she has no time to play at life, as some young people do. We gave her the gems from the king's treasure for a reason, and now it is time for her to learn the reason." The wizard stood and walked across to the opening in the castle wall. His dark blue robes fell in smooth folds that were reminiscent of the ocean as he walked. The garments settled around him as he stood and looked out over the Lincolnshire countryside. The sun was just setting, and the rolling green landscape sparkled with the last rays of light. Jonathan could see the past and future of this land as he gazed out, but just now he chose to see the land in the year 1216, just after the death of King John. Even though those in the magic world had anticipated the old king's death, they had removed his treasure from the material world as the wagon carrying it had crossed the Wash. Individual gems had been given to magic folk throughout the realm, and individual tasks would be assigned to each person who received a gem. The young girl Brianna had been given three, a red one, a green, and a yellow, which she sewed into the hem of her skirt. She had passed the first test. She understood the importance of the gems and kept them safe. But now the situation was changing. Rowena was dying.

And Michael was in Wales. Although he had not been given a gem, he would soon know who he really was, and what his tasks would be. Michael's great strengths were his compassion, which he showed to the girl Brianna, and his openness. He was open to the magic.

*****

Brianna sat across the small wooden table from Rowena, who watched as the girl unpicked stitching in the hem of her skirt and removed the gems. They were not small gems; each was about the size of the nail on Brianna's forefinger. They sparkled in the sunlight that streamed through the open door as she handed them to the older woman. Rowena was still strong. The disease that would soon bring about her death was little in evidence yet. There was only a look in her eyes that showed that she had begun to look to the next world. And Brianna often heard her friend, because she was now her friend as well as her mentor, pacing the small room during the night. Then she would doze off and on during the day.

Rowena took the gems in the palm of her hand and studied them. "They are fine stones. And worth much more in magical hands than in those of King John and his greedy cohorts."

"What am I to do with them?" Brianna asked.

Rowena smiled at the girl. "You must always be doing something. You are too eager. Sometimes one must simply wait, and when the time comes, you will know what to do if you are properly prepared."

"Then what must I do to prepare?"

Rowena said nothing. Instead she stood and went to the small carved wooden chest that sat beside her sleeping pallet. She muttered some words that Brianna could not hear and opened the lid. There was a rustling sound as she removed an object and then closed the lid soundlessly. When she returned to the table, she held something cupped between her hands which she set onto the table. It appeared to be a small birds' nest, as small as that of a wren, perhaps. But instead of the usual sticks and plant matter ordinarily found in a birds' next, this one was made of a white material, like snowflakes, but not snowflakes that would melt at a human touch. Rowena removed her hands from the nest. "Touch it. Put your hands around it as I did."

Brianna did as she was told, and felt the softness and warmth of the nest. "What is it? Is it a bird's nest?"

"It is," Rowena replied. "I have had it in my possession for many years."

"But what kind of a bird? I've never seen such a thing before. Where did you get it?"

Rowena laughed, but Brianna noticed that the laugh was not quite as joyful as it had been. "You ask so many questions, Brianna. It is good to be curious, but sometimes blurting out questions can lead to trouble." She wrapped her own hands around Brianna's as she held the nest. "I can't answer your questions now, but I can tell you what you need to know about this nest, and why I am giving it to you." The older woman looked around the cottage, seeming to wonder where she was, or else seeing her home with new eyes. "Pour us some more tea, Brianna. Teaching magic can be thirsty work."

After Brianna refreshed both of their mugs with the fragrant tea that Rowena made from mint and lemon verbena, she sat and waited for Rowena to begin. She had so many questions, but she curbed her tongue and instead sipped the tea, which calmed her curiosity and restlessness somewhat.

At last Rowena spoke. "At this time you have several magical objects in your possession. You have the jewels from King John's treasure, which were magically given to you. The possession of these jewels places a great deal of trust and confidence in you from the magical world. It also places you in great danger in the human world. Although no one would suspect that a common girl like you would be carrying the dead king's jewels in her skirt, just the fact that you have such items places you in peril. How else could you have acquired them except through theft?"

Brianna opened her mouth to speak, but Rowena silenced her with a smile and a raised hand, a silent reminder of what she had told her before. "Now you also possess this nest of the snow wren. This bird is like you. It lives in the world of mortal creatures, but has a magical life as well. This nest was given to me by a family of wrens who had finished with it for the season. If you know anything about wrens, you know they are feisty and very protective of their nests. But through magic, I was able to explain to these birds how their nest would be of great value to you on your magical quest."

"You got the nest for me?" Brianna could not restrain herself from speaking. "And what magical quest? I didn't know I was on a quest!"

Rowena smiled and did not this time reprimand Brianna for her questions. "I have had this nest for many years, that is years in human reckoning. I have known that you would be coming to me, although I did not know for sure who you were or when you would come. When the news came that

King John's treasure had been lost in the Wash through the folly of his human minions, the entire magical world was laughing, because, of course, we have it. It was simply spirited away as the wagon crossed the inlet of the North Sea. A king who thinks of nothing but his own desires and waging war has no business possessing such a fortune. Some day England may be worthy of these jewels again. But then again, the nation may reach the point where the rulers and citizens realize that jewels are not necessary to live well."

Brianna stared at the woman across the table from her. Could this be true? But it still didn't explain why she had the stones. Uncharacteristically, she could think of nothing to say.

"Your quest began as a simple one. You wanted to find your mother. I'm afraid we have taken advantage of your wishes. We knew that you would leave the village, which happens to be quite near the Wash where the treasure was supposedly lost. And it was for your safety as well. Andera argued strongly for you to be brought to the magical world, where you could be taught what your mother had failed to teach you. Your magic is strong, Brianna, much stronger than you realize." Rowena reached down absently to stroke the back of Orangino, who had come in the door, recognizing that his dinner time was approaching. The sun had moved lower in the sky, and the breeze that wafted through the door was cool, the light golden.

"But only my mother is magic," Brianna countered. "My father is mortal, so how can my magic be that strong? You have said that my mother never developed her powers."

"This is probably the most important piece of information that you lack, Brianna. I have discussed this with the folk in the magic dimension and they agree that it is time you were told. Your father most definitely is magic, Brianna. But he did not and still does not know. Neither did you mother have any idea. She thought that by having a

139

relationship with a mortal and giving birth to a mixed child, she was rebelling against her magical family in the strongest way possible. But her rebellion backfired, because your father most definitely possesses magic, which he is only learning about right now."

The room was darkening, but neither of them rose to light a candle. Orangino had settled next to the fireplace where embers smoldered throughout the day, realizing that his supper must wait until the humans had finished their conversation. He had enjoyed a field mouse not long ago, which had taken the edge off his hunger.

"Where is my father?" Brianna whispered. Rowena waited so long to respond that she doubted that the older woman had heard her and was about to repeat the question.

"It is not yet time for you to have that information," Rowena finally answered in a strong, firm voice, stronger than her voice had been throughout the entire conversation. "It is enough for you to know that he exists; he is magic, and you will meet him when the time is right." She stood and walked to the doorway to close the door. "Orangino is hungry. There are some bits of the rabbit that we enjoyed yesterday in that crock. Give him some of that."

Brianna obeyed and watched for a minute as the orange cat tucked into his meal with the combination of pleasure and delicacy that only cats can exhibit. Only after several minutes had passed, did she look up and see that Rowena was still standing in the doorway, looking out into the night. "Is something wrong?"

"No. Nothing is wrong. But the magic is strong in the air tonight, and I'm not sure why it is so strong." When Brianna joined her at the door, Rowena slipped her arm around the young girl's waist. "Breathe in. Feel it," she said.

Brianna inhaled deeply and was surprised to feel the power that surged through her. She exhaled and the power, the feeling of strength, remained. She turned to face Rowena, and for the first time realized how much taller she was than the older woman. Had she grown? Or had the other woman shrunk with age and illness? "Take another breath," Rowena told her.

Brianna did as she was told and although the power did not seem to increase, it seemed to solidify within her. When she exhaled the power remained. "Very good. That's enough for tonight." Orangino, having finished his supper, slipped past them out into the night. Rowena closed the door softly and slipped the bar into place. "We could leave the door open tonight and be in no danger from mortals or magicians, but it is best to follow our habits, so we don't forget in the future. There will undoubtedly be nights in the future that will not be as safe as this one."

Chapter 24

"There is nothing that moves a loving father's soul quite
like his child's cry."

Jonathani Eareckson Tada

Magic Realm

"I think we need to get Brianna to her father, or him to
her," Andera said. They had been over this argument in the
great room of Lincoln Castle many times. No one could see
them, of course, because they were not in the same time
dimension as the residents of the castle in the Year of Our
Lord 1216. The magical coven of Lincoln used the great
room for important discussion when they all needed to
gather. The living quarters for the folk who lived in the castle
were in the rooms above. It was simple, really. All they had
to do was take up residence wherever they wanted to live,
and create a time shift. Then they were living in one time in
English history, while the world around them was in another.
Sometimes humans who were sensitive to magic would be
aware of their presence, and that was how the stories of
ghosts came about. There were no ghosts. It was simply
magic folks living in another time dimension.

"She still has much to learn from Rowena. The woman
is not as near death as some of you seem to believe." The old
man looked around at the group who lounged on comfortable
embroidered chairs and simple wooden benches. Some
sipped tea out of china cups; others quaffed mead from

142

earthenware goblets. Their clothing, too, reflected different time periods. The women tended to favor the flowing skirts of what historians called the Middle Ages, while the men opted for the comfort of the trousers that had replaced the short pants and hose around the beginning of the nineteenth century. One young man had shown up in the blue jeans and T-shirt that would be in style in the late twentieth century, but was sent back to change with the admonition that he had gone too far. There was a sense of dignity and decorum that must be maintained.

"And then there is Marged," the young man who had dared to wear jeans interjected. "That woman is a loose cannon." They all stared at him, pondering his choice of words. "I mean . . ." he shifted on the bench where he was sitting but did not stand. "You never know what she will do. Her judgment is poor. She should be learning from Rowena," he finished.

"You are right about Marged," the old wizard Jonathan said, "and I say that with full knowledge of my daughter. There is a real risk that she could put her own daughter Brianna in serious danger, which is one of the reasons I strengthened the magic around Rowena's cottage tonight."

"But Marged is confined to Dover Castle, is she not?" The question was asked by Sinead, a beautiful woman with long white blonde hair and turquoise eyes, who held an infant to her breast.

"She is," the old man answered. "We sent her to the middle of the twentieth century and set a spell to confine her in the oldest part of the castle, but she was able to get around it, as I knew she would. She has been taunting the soldiers on duty there."

"Ah. Another war," the young mother said, snuggling her infant closer.

"Yes. Another war," Andera repeated. "But that doesn't seem to stop Marged from having fun and flirting with young men, even if they do think she is a ghost."

"If she can escape the locking spell on the oldest part of the castle, can she leave the castle itself? And does she know enough to travel to a different time?" Sinead asked.

"That is what we are worried about," answered an older woman whose thick gray hair was pulled back from a still beautiful face, with high cheek bones and piercing blue eyes. "And if she does escape, where and when will she go? She could bring danger to more than herself and her daughter."

"Can't we just bring her back here?" A male voice from the back of the crowd asked.

"We could," Jonathan answered. "But in her case a little knowledge of magic is more than dangerous, it could be deadly. If we try to control her too tightly, the situation may backfire."

"Our most important goal here," Rhys, mother of Andera and Marged, added, "is to protect Brianna and to train her in magic ways. Brianna has power and integrity, two valuable commodities in a magic person. Our second goal is to be sure that the king's treasure is well hidden, until such time as humanity can handle such riches, or until the need is greatest."

"But what is the use of gold and jewels except to show off wealth, or to sell for something else?" asked Sinead, whose baby had now fallen asleep on her shoulder.

"Exactly," Rhys replied. "But few humans know that, and not all magical people do either."

Chapter 25

"It is good to have an end to journey toward; but it is the journey that matters, in the end."

Ernest Hemingway

The Brecon Beacons, Wales

Michael and young Mory did indeed reach the Brecon Beacons, a mountain range in south Wales, and began to climb. The wind chilled them as they wound up the narrow paths. It was not yet winter, but the darkening sky and swirling leaves told them that they were well into fall. The families in the remote cottages nestled in the valleys welcomed them, as they had been told they would. Michael listened to his companion explaining their purpose in rapid Welsh, and wondered if they were laughing at him, the Englishman. They did not seem to fear him, but why would they? As Mory's father had said, "What would an Englishman who speaks no Welsh be doing alone in Wales unless he were running from the English?"

As the days passed, Michael began to pick up a few words of Welsh, or Cymraeg as it was in that language. He and Mory passed the time as they rode with language lessons, and soon Michael was able to understand and extend simple greetings, and basic questions and answers. The subtleties of the language eluded him, however. He had traveled on the Continent of Europe and as far as the Holy Land, and spoke French and Italian well, and a smattering of Eastern languages, but Welsh was like nothing he had heard before. A simple "thank you" was "diolch i chi" in Welsh, an almost impossible mouthful for an Englishman.

He could see that Mory took seriously his father's proposal that he search for a wife among the families that they visited, and although they had met a few young girls of the right age, lovely and smiling with dark hair and flashing eyes, none seemed to appeal to Mory in more than a flirtatious way.

It was now the third week of their travels, and they had ridden through the rain all day, with little energy for practicing Welsh. The sky was dark, and they could not discern when the day was near its end except for the tiredness they felt after so many hours on horseback. The trail had turned to mud and the horses slowed their steps, heads down. When the ruins of a Roman fort came into view, Michael slowed his mount and pointed ahead to Mory. "Let's find shelter here. We risk the horses stumbling if we go farther. Who knows where the next cottage will be?"

"Right." Mory answered. He looked dubiously at the dark stones amid the trees and seemed about to object, but his fatigue, hunger and discomfort in his clothes which were now soaked through changed his mind. They dismounted and led the horses through the vegetation to the stone outcroppings that had once been an outpost of the Roman Empire. With the roofs long gone, the old fort offered little in the way of protection from the elements, but the remains of a tower, probably used as a lookout post, had retained some covering, and it was wide enough at the base that they were able to bring the horses inside. The animals seemed just as happy as Michael and Mory were to be in out of the unrelenting rain.

"We can't build a fire," Michael said as they rubbed down the horses, and were rewarded with appreciative snickers. "There is no dry kindling, and the smoke would drive us out of here if we could start a fire."

"It's all right," Mory answered, stifling a yawn. "It's reasonably dry and should be safe." The boy's eyes scanned the high walls of the tower. "Who would look for us in such a place on a rainy night?"

They pulled packets of oats from their saddlebags, which had managed to stay dry. Normally, they liked to allow the horses to graze, but they carried oats for just such emergencies when there was little or nothing for the animals to eat. Once the horses were munching contentedly from their nosebags, Michael and Mory set about making sleeping arrangements for themselves. The earth floor was dry, although the humidity and dampness pervaded everything they touched. They each lay out their bedding close to the walls, one on each side of the horses. To satisfy their hunger, the travelers had to be content with a little bread and cheese from the last farmhouse they had visited. "We need to save a little for morning," Michael commented. "I only hope the rain will stop by then."

Mory produced a handful of nuts that he had gathered the previous morning before the rain began, and added them to their meal. The boy continued to scan the upper reaches of the tower with a concerned face, but Michael assumed he was worried about water making its way into their shelter if the storm grew worse. The older man lay down, preparing to sleep. It was almost impossible to see in the enclosed structure, and he was exhausted from the day. Once again, he was aware of Mory looking up into the darkness. "What do you see up there, Mory?" he asked finally.

"Nothing," the boy replied. "I hope nothing."

"What do you mean? 'You hope nothing.'"

"Spirits," Mory answered. "Spirits take refuge in these old buildings sometimes. I don't want to disturb them." The boy spoke in such a matter of fact manner that Michael wasn't sure he was serious. It was the first time on their journey that he had spoken of such things, although Michael knew that the Welsh even more than the English believed in supernatural beings. "They won't bother us," Mory said at last. He lay down and was soon asleep.

Michael lay awake in the darkness, listening to the rain, the soft breathing of the boy, and the shuffling and gentle snorts of the horses. Nothing else disturbed them. It seemed to be only seconds later that he woke. Dim light had seeped into their haven, and Mory was no longer in the tower. The horses still stood peacefully, and one snickered when Michael stood up. He stepped outside to relieve himself and found that the sun had broken through the clouds. It promised to be a fine clear day, although cold. He had just finished when a sound from the other side of the tower made him start. Mory burst through the underbrush, a huge grin on his face and a small package in his hands.

"They were good spirits. Look." He opened the package to reveal a couple of oatcakes and good Welsh cheese, along with two apples.

"Where did you get that?" Michael's mouth watered at the sight of the food.

"Just here." He pointed to the entrance to the tower from which Michael had just emerged.

"Then what were you doing on the other side?"

"I heard something, and I thought they might be there. I wanted to thank them for the food."

Michael did not know what to say. The boy was practical and intelligent, that he knew from their days of traveling. This was the first time he had spoken of spirits in the woods, and while it was not an unusual belief among country folk, it still surprised Michael. "Do you really think spirits brought this?" he asked as he picked up an oatcake and took a bite. "This cake seems quite solid to me, and likely made by human hands."

Mory smiled. "I know. But in a place like this, on a night like last night, it's best to consider all the possibilities. At least that what my Da says. My granny now. She believes in spirits. She says she sees them all the time."

"Have you ever seen any?"

"Naw." The boy broke off a hunk of cheese. "But I keep an open mind. And where do you think this food came from?" He grinned impishly.

"I don't know." Michael's eyes scanned the forest around them, and the stone ruins in which they stood. "I really don't know, but I am grateful to whoever brought us this gift. I have seen enough that is strange in the world to know that there is much we do not know." He thought of Rowena the witch and the girl Brianna. There was certainly something about them that was not of this world. And Brianna reminded him of someone, someone from his past. She had a magnetism that drew him to protect her. He hope she was safe.

A snicker from within the tower reminded them of their duties, and they left off talk of spirits to tend to the horses and prepare for the day. Michael had a sense that they were nearing their destination, and he was eager to ride on this bright autumn day.

In the light of day, the dark Roman ruins and the forest surrounding them did not have nearly the ominous sense of foreboding that both Michael and Mory had felt the night before, although neither had admitted their feelings to the other. And without speaking, both felt that they were nearing the end of their journey. Michael wondered if the boy was disappointed that he had not yet met a young woman he could take as a wife. He had begun to think of Mory's search as the focus of their journey, rather than his own search for . . . what? He was evading the English soldiers that would no doubt be looking for him after his involvement in the battle in which James, the innkeeper from Worcester, had been killed. And he was known to associate with the witch Brianna. His heart caught in his throat as he thought of what could happen if she were captured and tried as a witch. Not that the trial would have any aspect of justice to it. A common method to determine guilt in a witchcraft trial was to throw the accused woman -- and it was almost always a woman -- into the nearest body of water. If she sank and drowned, she was innocent. Poor woman, may God rest her soul. If she floated or by some chance was able to swim, this unnatural ability showed her guilt, and she would be burned at the stake, the most horrible death one could imagine.

But Rowena told him to flee to Wales, that he would be safe here. And there was something he was supposed to learn in this place, although he had no idea what, other than the Welsh language, and he couldn't see what earthly good that would do him once he returned to England. And he would return, of that he was certain. If nothing else, he would have to reassure himself that Brianna and Rowena were well. He had spent his life as a knight, traveling around Europe and to the Holy Land, living by his wits and fighting for the king of England, first Richard I, may God rest his soul, and then his brother John, who had not inspired the loyalty of his subjects and had now gone to his heavenly reward as well. As Sir Michael he would return to fight in the service of the new boy king, John's son. He was known at court, and knew no other life.

The trail led upwards for an hour's ride, until the trees began to thin out toward the summit. Just as they expected to come out into the sunlight, the trail veered sharply to the left and plunged back down into the forest. Here it leveled off and continued, a serene, leafy path, softened by a carpet of fallen leaves. The sunlight shown through the branches overhead, making the light play tricks on their eyes. A movement in the road ahead caused the horses to shy, but on examination it proved to be only a breeze stirring the bright yellow leaves. Michael and Mory dismounted to lead the horses through this strange wood. Michael was fully alert, one hand on his horse's bridle and the other on the hilt of his sword. Mory, too, seemed wary, his head swiveling from side to side, scanning for anything that might portend danger. An unearthly laugh echoed overhead, and both men stopped, hearts pounding, until they spotted a mockingbird coming to rest in a tree just before a bend in the trail a few yards in front of them. Michael and Mory looked at each other and both laughed themselves, but their laughter was blended with a fearful tension that neither was willing to admit.

They were unable to see what was around the bend, and Michael silently indicated that he would lead the way. The two remounted their horses, and Michael removed his sword from its scabbard, ready to do battle with whatever might be waiting for them. There was no tangible threat, but the air was full of menace. He rode on around the bend, and then beckoned for Mory to follow. There was nothing in sight but the same trail, the same trees, with their yellow leaves falling underfoot. Some distance ahead the path turned to the left again, and the mockingbird was just visible on a low branch just before the bend. It gave a call and flew off into the distance and disappeared.

Michael took a deep breath, but did not remove his hand from the hilt of his sword. The feeling of menace had dissipated somewhat, but Michael knew as a soldier that it was always wise to rely on more than your feelings. You had to also keep your wits about you. He slowed his horse to a quiet walk and motioned for Mory to do the same. The trail was descending now, and they seemed to be going back the way they had come. Michael wondered if they might have become lost last night in the storm and taken a wrong turn. But if the trail led downward, they would eventually find a village or some habitation. He had no desire to turn around and travel through that eerie path again.

The trail grew steep and at times seemed to almost disappear. Just when they thought they had lost it altogether, they smelled smoke. Smoke meant one thing -- habitation. Michael guessed they had somehow lost the trail and found it again, or were approaching a village or, more likely, an isolated farm, from the other direction. There was probably a much more direct path from below, and they could have avoided spending the night in drafty Roman ruins and traveling a haunted path this morning.

A dog barked -- a sure sign that their approach had been heard. Michael sincerely hoped they would be welcome, and perhaps even be offered breakfast. That would be the normal procedure in welcoming strangers in this part of the world, but after the unearthly sensations of the morning's ride, he wasn't sure what rules might apply.

When they finally emerged into the clearing, the two riders found that they were not at an isolated homestead as they expected, but instead they found a stone building that looked like a meeting place of some kind. A dozen men on horseback milled around, the horses champing at the bit, ready for a morning's ride.

"Ah. You are here at last." A tall man wearing a red cape called to the newcomers. He had been about to mount his horse when he saw Michael and Mory, and stopped to come to greet them. "The boy will stay here," he said, indicating Mory. "You," and he pointed a long finger at Michael, "will ride with us."

"Who are you?" Michael's words were lost in the shuffle as riders whistled and horses neighed.

A rider nearly as young as Mory handed Michael an oatcake. "Marc always forgets that not everyone can go without food the way he can. We will stop later but this will get you by until then."

"But . . ." Michael had no chance to ask questions as he was surrounded by the riders and given no alternative but to move out with them.

Mory found the bridle of his horse held by a boy about his age, so he could not have joined the group riding out even if he were inclined to. His chances for breakfast were better if he remained at the camp, if that was what it was. Nevertheless, he was watched in dismay as Michael was coerced into riding out, and wondered what they had gotten themselves into. Was it a deliberate attempt to separate them? And why? Mory's father had said they would be safe, so they would just have to trust. And at the moment, what choice did they have?

Mory tore his eyes away from the backs of the riders, who were quickly disappearing into the forest, and looked down. He shook his head, thinking he was seeing double, when he saw two pairs of eyes in identical smiling faces looking up at him, only by their clothing did he determine that one was a boy and one a girl. "Come in and have some breakfast." The girl's voice sounded like flowing water. "Your friend will be back later. Don't worry about him."

Again, Mory had no choice, so he dismounted and tied his horse with another outside the door of the stone building. "Are you twins?" he asked as he turned to follow them indoors.

They both laughed, hers as musical as a flute, his lower but with the same sound of joy and life. "We are," the girl replied. "I am Loa and this is my brother Robert."

"I am Mory," he said.

"We know," Robert answered quickly. "We have been expecting you. Come in. Our Ma has prepared some food. I know you are hungry."

A selection of bread, cheese, and fruit was laid out on the wooden table, and the twins indicated that Mory should help himself to what he wanted. He looked around for their mother, whom they said had prepared the food. He wanted to offer his greetings and his thanks, as he had been taught to do. "Where is your mother?"

Again he heard the musical laughter from the two of them. "Oh, she's not here," Loa replied. "She just sent the food. Go on. Eat."

Mory piled his plate high with food, with the twins encouraging him. They refused to take any themselves, claiming they had already eaten. But the bread was too soft and fresh, the fruit too ripe and sweet, for Mory to resist. It had been days since his stomach had felt full, and he had never tasted food like this, although his mother was an excellent cook, and the fruit trees on their farm produced peaches and cherries that melted in one's mouth. Loa and Robert sat at the table and watched him, giggling occasionally at some secret joke. When he had cleaned his plate, they motioned for him to take a second helping, and although the serving plates appeared as full as they had been at the beginning, Mory found that he could not move from his seat. His eyelids dropped and his head would have fallen onto his plate if Loa had not moved it and substituted a small blanket to cushion his head. The twins smiled at each other in silent complicity and left him alone.

Chapter 26

"Let me not pray to be sheltered from dangers,
but to be fearless in facing them.
Let me not beg for the stilling of my pain, but
for the heart to conquer it."

Rabindranath Tagore, *Collected Poems and Plays of
Rabindranath Tagore*

"So you have buried the witch." The voice was filled
with menace. "Now all we have to do is bury you. And
without her to protect you, it will be easy. Fortunately for us,
she did not have time to teach you all she knows. So you are
what? Half a witch? That's not much better than no witch at
all, but enough to warrant a witch's death."

Brianna gasped for breath. Who was speaking to her?
She woke to see the sunlight just creeping through the cracks
in Rowena's cottage. Orangino sat at the foot of her bed,
staring at her with his inscrutable gaze. The voice in her
nightmare spoke the truth. She had buried her friend and
mentor, Rowena, the day before. With the help of the
villagers who had known Rowena for so long, they laid her
to rest next to her husband from long ago, and the innkeeper
James, who had died protecting Brianna. Now she was alone
again, and in danger again. She felt as she had before she left
the village where she had grown up, so far away next to the
fens. She still had Orangino looking out for her, but he was
a cat. He could protect her, warn her of danger and let her
know when all was well and she could rest, but he could not
give her the counsel that she so badly needed. Should she

remain in the village or go? It was the second time she had been faced with this dilemma. "Andera," she whispered. "Where are you? I need your help?" The cottage remained still, with only the sound of the birds outside the door. *If only I could go to the magic world*, Brianna thought. *I could find my mother. I could be safe.* Her connections in the magic world were silent.

On a practical, worldly level, she knew she needed to leave the village. But where would she go? She rose and stretched her arms over her head. Rowena had told her to breath and trust. When she was unsure of her direction -- breathe and trust -- and the answer would come. She went outside in the chill early morning, followed closely by Orangino. She washed her face in the cold water Rowena had always kept for that purpose and rubbed her face dry with an old cloth. Cleanliness. Start with cleanliness. She rinsed her mouth and rubbed a sprig of mint on her teeth to freshen her breath. Orangino returned from his morning foray into the trees and rubbed against her leg. She bent to rub his back and discovered that he held something in his mouth. "What have you got now, Orangino?" she asked. "Drop it." He didn't drop it. He was enough of a non-magical cat to not obey the directive of a human if it didn't suit him, but he did allow her to remove the object from between his jaws.

"Where did you get this?" A large ruby, about the size of the head of a mouse, fell into her hand. The cat continued to rub against Brianna's legs. She would get no answer from the cat, but she knew without a doubt that the ruby was also part of King John's lost treasure, and she knew it had come into her possession through magic. Was it from Rowena? Or from the same source that had brought her the jewels that lay sewn inside her skirt? Whatever its origin, it only increased her personal danger. The voice in her dream was a warning; she had no doubt about that. And she needed to leave this village where the people had been so kind to her because of her friendship with Rowena. They had protected her and treated her as one of them, knowing all the time that she possessed magical powers. But she was not Rowena. She had another destiny, although she wasn't sure what it was. She needed to go. Where had Sir Michael gone? Wales. Perhaps she should go to Wales as well. Rowena had said that Michael would be safe there. Perhaps she would be safe as well. She would spend the day preparing to leave. Tomorrow morning at first light, she would be gone. She and Orangino would head toward Wales.

As she sorted through the belongings that she would take with her, she found the boy's clothing that she had worn on her escape from London so many months ago. She would need to wear it again. A girl would not be traveling alone, and whoever was looking for her would be asking about a girl. And she would cut her hair tonight. She would take no chances on hiding her long hair through magic as she had when she fled Worcester on horseback. She did not want any of the villagers to know her plans until after she had gone. It wasn't that she didn't trust them, but they could be in danger, too. Her next task was to take all of the jewels and cover them with a thick coat of clay. When it hardened, they would look like rough stones, nothing of value at all. If they were found, it might protect her for a little while if it were thought that she carried only stones. It was the best she could do. She would have to rely on magic and her wits after that.

None of the villagers visited her that day as she made her preparations. She thought they would not. She was not Rowena, and maybe they believed that she would leave. They would not be willing to protect her and take her into their care as they had the old woman. She looked around the small cottage that had been Rowena's home. She had shared it with her for only a few months, but the old woman had made her feel that it was her home -- more than her home.

She had made Brianna feel like a daughter. Brianna loved her own mother, but her relationship with the witch Rowena was very different. Brianna's own mother Marged had been a girl herself, and although she did her best to teach Brianna how to live, she was too disorganized and flighty to be consistent in her instruction. Rowena was the opposite. She was aware that they had limited time together; therefore, she used the time with efficiency. She taught her magic, how to control her mind and reach out to the spirit world when she needed to. She taught her to be honest and truthful and kind, because only with those virtues could she accomplish what she was put on this earth to do. She taught her about the use of plants for healing, and other more esoteric uses as well. She told her of the dangers to be aware of, and how to know what was in a person's mind by their body language. They would both have liked to have more time, but some things cannot be changed. And as Rowena slipped from this life, she taught Brianna not to fear death, that is was only a transition to the next life.

Brianna packed a few of the herbs in Rowena's supply for her journey. There was little enough of material possessions in the cottage. Rowena had not cared for those things. Brianna searched for some small item that would remind her of this special woman and the days she had spent here, but there was nothing that had particular meaning. She wanted something that would hold the essence of Rowena, but everything that she picked up fell short. The herbs themselves? The frayed blanket she had used to cover Brianna her first night in the cottage? The mortar and pestle, well-used and chipped, that she used to grind herbs? Brianna finally settled on the last. In her mind's eye, she could the old woman using her strength and long practice to press against the seeds and leaves in the stone mortar. It was nothing, really. But it was useful, and maybe some of Rowena's strength would be transferred to Brianna through this simple stone object. And she still has the knife that she had been given in Newark. It could come in useful, but she hoped not. A situation requiring a knife was a situation Brianna would avoid at all costs.

When she was ready for the journey, Brianna lovingly tended the garden next to the cottage, pulling weeds and pinching off the heads so the plants who grow full and lush. She wondered what would happen to the garden and the cottage once she was gone? Someone would surely want to live in it. There was a shortage of housing in the village, and newly-wed couples often were forced to live with the parents of the husband or wife. Or would there be a stigma attached to the house that had belonged to the village witch?

When the gardening was done, Brianna lay down to rest. She intended to rise well before dawn to be on her way, and be far from the village by the time anyone realized she was gone. Orangino curled up next to her on Rowena's narrow pallet in the corner, but Brianna could not relax. As much as she needed sleep, she was restless. After tossing and turning, and disturbing her patient cat time and time again, she gave up on rest. She checked her supplies once again. And as the sun began its journey toward twilight, she visited the graves of Rowena, her husband, and James the innkeeper one last time. After whispering a prayer to whatever god might be listening, she turned back to the cottage. She was ready. Orangino sat just outside the door, alert and ready for something. "It's not time for your supper yet," she said to him. He continued to stare at her as she went inside. She felt the presence as soon as she entered, but could not see who it was until her eyes adjusted.

"It's only me," a soft feminine voice announced. "Andera."

Brianna smiled at the woman she knew now was her aunt. "I'm so happy to see you."

Andera stood and embraced the girl. "You have done well since I last saw you."

"I've gone from one scrape to the next, but I've survived. I have been helped by wonderful people, but I have to leave here now. Rowena is dead."

"I know," Andera's voice was sad.

"Of course you know." Brianna smiled at this woman whom she had grown to love. "You are magic. You know everything that goes on."

"Not everything," Andera laughed. "But since I have been put in charge of your training, I do know what goes on in your life." She looked around the room. "I see you are preparing to go."

"Yes. I can't stay here. I could put the villagers in danger, and it isn't safe for me either."

"You mentioned the villagers first. That is admirable. You put yourself last."

Brianna blushed. "I hadn't thought about it."

"That's why it is admirable. Rowena has taught you well, but you were a good student to begin with."

"I thought I would travel toward Wales," Brianna twisted the hem of her sleeve as she spoke, a sure sign of her lack of certainty in her decision.

Andera noticed and the corners of her mouth twitched. "Because that is where Michael went, and Rowena told him it would be safe for him."

"Yes. It was the best I could think of. Did I make the right choice?"

"You did. Wales is a safe place for magic folk. And the deeper into the country you go, the safer you will be. You will not see Michael yet, however. It's not time."

"But will I see him again? I liked him!" Brianna felt a tug at her heart at the thought of never seeing that kind man again, whatever his name and whether or not he was a knight in the service of the king.

"Oh, yes! You will see him. You are destined to see him again."

Chapter 27

Life is either a daring adventure or nothing at all."

Helen Keller, *The Open Door*

Brianna cut her hair by moonlight, as her mother had taught her to do. She had said it made the hair more receptive to separation from the body. Brianna wasn't sure about this, as she wasn't sure about much that her mother had told her, but it was a good time, after the villagers were all asleep. She tied the cuttings into a small cloth and left them on the table. She didn't dare risk throwing them on the fire. The smell and the sight of a fire burning brightly rather than coals glowing in the night could attract the attention of wakeful villagers. She dressed in the boy's clothing that she had worn on her arrival, and tied an improvised knapsack around her shoulders to carry a few items -- a large cloth that could serve as a skirt if the time came for her to dress as a girl once again, some bread, cheese and dried fruit, oats for her horse and for her own stomach as well if need be. She had Orangino's traveling sack in which he had snuggled next to her on the journey with Michael out of Worcester on that night so long ago. She wrapped the mortar and pestle in a square of rough cloth and tied it to the saddle. Thanks to Rowena, she was confident now riding Belle. She did not consider herself an expert horsewoman, but she was not afraid as she had been.

It was still dark when she looked around the single room for the last time. There were no "good-byes" to say. That had been done the day they had buried Rowena. Her spirit was not tied to any earthly location, and Brianna knew that the old woman would be there for her when she was needed. Orangino was ready. He had undoubtedly spent the night hunting and his stomach was full. Besides the cover of darkness, Brianna was most grateful for a sturdy pair of boots on this autumn morning. Rowena had seen that the village cobbler had made a good leather pair for her before she died, sensing that Brianna would need them not far in the future. She mounted the horse with Orangino safely in front of her, and rode through the sleeping village, taking the road west toward Wales. If anyone in the village saw her go, they would not stop her, of that she was sure.

The road was quiet, and she rode steadily as the sun came up behind her. She didn't know exactly where she was headed, or how long it would take her to reach her destination. She was headed toward Wales because that was where Sir Michael had gone. If it was safe for him, it would be safe for her.

Although Brianna was safely on the road, she had only narrowly escaped danger in the village she had just left. Men claiming to be emissaries of the King arrived in the village barely a day after Brianna and Orangino departed. It was only due to sheer luck that they did not harm to the villagers, although they did rough up some of the young men a bit, but they burnt Rowena's small cottage to the ground. They found the bag of hair, but, not thinking that it belonged to a girl who was traveling in disguise as a boy, took it as a sign of magic and burnt it along with the house.

None of the villagers could say where she had gone because they didn't know. All the villagers knew was that the old witch had died, and the knight who had arrived with the young girl was long gone, too. They did wonder why it took so long for anyone to arrive from London, since it had been many months since the girl arrived, but the visitors told them simply that things had been chaotic in London since the death of King John and the accession of the new boy king.

But a case of witchcraft was not forgotten. There had even been rumors from the manor of a local landholder that acts of the devil had been seen by some of the young boys. One of the soldiers, younger than the rest, even asked questions about the orange cat. The villagers replied that there were many cats in a village such as theirs, and pointed out a grey one that sauntered away from the witch's house and disappeared into the woods. "Never mind, Thomas," the leader of the soldiers called out. "They aren't here, and I'm not taking time to chase a cat."

Brianna had no inkling of such things as she made her way west. She did her best to travel by night, and clung to the side of the roads for fear of being seen by peasants working the land. She was young and strong and full of energy, and was able to cover good distances every night. She slept little, usually early in the morning before first light, before anyone was likely to be out and about. During the day, she hid -- in a woods surrounded by trees, in the branches of a tree if it were possible. Once she found a cave, probably dug out by an animal, next to a stream, and huddled there for the daylight hours, feeling safe from humans, but fearful all the time that the animal who created the cave might return. She continued to rely on Orangino. Although there was little he could do to actually protect her, his demeanor told her if there was danger in the area. As long as he was serenely sitting about, cleaning his fur and resting, his eyelids drooping, she felt safe.

She had almost reached the market town of Swindon when she sensed the first sign of trouble. The sign was when Orangino clung to her side switching his tale when she was trying to settle in for her day's rest, and her horse whinnied restlessly. But it was not riders from the king's court who threatened her journey; there were sounds in the woods that were most definitely human, but they were not searching for a young girl disguised as a boy. Soon she and Orangino heard shouts of laughter and excitement as men, women and children ran through the trees, gathering fallen dry sticks. Brianna had hidden herself well in a hole in the trunk of an old oak tree, and her cat crouched in front of her just inside the entrance, emitting a low growl as the people moved closer to their hiding place. She had tethered the horse in a dense thicket nearby, and whispered a "hiding" spell as the villagers moved through the wood. Just as suddenly, the crowd of people disappeared, carrying their armloads of dry sticks. Orangino stopped his growling but stayed at the alert, his tail switching back and forth. Eventually Brianna relaxed and dozed. The danger, if there was any, seemed to be gone, and it wasn't directed against her anyway. She woke with a start and realized that night had fallen. She had slept soundly, and her limbs and back were cramped from remaining in the tight, small space for so long. Orangino was nowhere to be seen. Brianna heard nothing in the surrounding woods save the hoot of an owl and the rustling of small rodents in the undergrowth. She unwound herself out of the hole in the tree and stood up. She breathed slowly, allowing her senses to take in everything in her surroundings, in both the physical and spirit worlds. Physically, she felt safe. Orangino was around somewhere close, of that she was certain. But there was something, some disturbance in the atmosphere, the boundary that so delicately separated the human world from the magical one. She didn't sense evil, but at the same time she did not feel the loving, benign presence of Rowena or Andera. She waited a moment, but felt nothing different. As quietly as possible, she moved out of the woods to the path leading into the village. She had no intention of entering a populated area, even in the dark of night, but she would follow the path until she could skirt the town and continue on her journey west. She left her horse, still magically invisible in the thicket, until she had a chance to scout the road out of the village. Just as she has nearly reached the western edge of the small community, she heard the crack of a twig just ahead of her. She froze, and in the silence heard breathing. Her own? She held her breath and the breathing continued. Someone was there, and from the raggedness in the breath, it was someone just as afraid as she was. Her dagger was tucked in her boot. Tentatively she stepped forward, ready to run or strike if she must. She had not traveled ten steps when someone about her height stepped out of the shadows. "Who are you?" a voice hissed.

Brianna said nothing, but continued to walk forward. As she reached the person in the darkness, an arm shot out, and clasped her arm in an iron grip. "I said 'Who are you'?" the voice hissed again.

Brianna twisted her arm and kicked out with her leg. The grip loosened slightly, allowing her to twist again until she was face to face with her attacker. She could not see the facial features in the dark, but there was just enough moonlight to tell that the person was about her height, and judging from the strength of the grip, about her own age. A grown man would have been stronger, a woman or younger person weaker. And he or she was not an experienced fighter, or the grip would not have loosened.

"What do you want?" Brianna hissed in her own most threatening voice.

"I want to know who you are and why you are lurking here in the darkness. Are you another witch?"

Brianna nearly gasped aloud but caught herself. Another witch? "I'm searching for my father," she blurted. "My mother died recently, and she told me to travel toward Wales to find my father." (Surely Rowena would forgive her this lie. Rowena was a mother to her in some ways. But would her own mother forgive her? There was every chance that she would find out. She was magic, if an imperfect magical woman.)

"Then come with me," the voice insisted, tightening the grip on Brianna's arm once again. "We'll soon see if you tell the truth."

Brianna pulled again, but it was no use. She was being dragged toward the nearest cottages. "Come! Someone come! I've found someone in the woods! It could be another witch!" her captor shouted.

Brianna looked around desperately for Orangino, but could not see him in the dark. She thought she saw his eyes glowing deeper in the forest, but it could have been any animal, hunting in the night.

There were shouts from several cottages and other men who seemed to be awake and on guard in the village. Brianna gave one last pull against her captor and tried to kick again, anything to put him off guard and allow her to escape. But it was no use. Even if she could escape, there was every chance she would be caught again and treated more roughly. The villagers knew the terrain here, even in the dark of night, and she did not. There was no reason for them to hold her, nothing to connect her with witchcraft, only a few herbs, and everyone used herbs of various sorts for healing. She relaxed. She would not be deserted. She had been saved before by Orangino, by Andera, and by her own wits.

Torches were lit by the time her captors dragged Brianna into the center of the village. There was enough light for her to make out a small square with a ramshackle stone church on the other side. It might have been a pretty town in the daylight, and if Brianna were not terrified. On the side of the square opposite the church, she saw a wooden framework of some kind, and as she looked, there was movement. Someone was tied to the framework in what looked like a most uncomfortable position. The person, who appeared to be a woman, was bound in such a way that she was bent over one piece of wood with her hands outstretched and tied to the ends. "I see you've found her!" the woman cried in a hoarse voice. She was wracked by a fit of coughing, the effort of crying out while she was held in such a position proved to be too much. The men ignored her as they approached Brianna.

Brianna was now able to see who had accosted her in the woods outside the village. A young man about her own age, with dark brown hair that fell into his eyes, twisted her arm behind her back as he pushed her toward the group of men waiting to see who had been found. "A young lad," one of them cried. "What is your business here, and at night, to sneak in and murder us in our beds?"

Brianna tripped as she was shoved forward and suddenly released. There was no danger of her escaping now, and the young lad had done his duty in capturing her. She sprawled in a heap into the dust. Before she could catch her breath and climb to her feet, she was once more grabbed by the arm, but this time it was the grip of a burly man, and she would surely have bruises to show for it.

"State your business!" he shouted. "What are you doing lurking in the night around our village?"

Brianna coughed and bent forward. She coughed again as she stood, remembering just in time to lower her voice to the level at least of a half-grown lad. "I travel at night for safety. My mother died, and I'm on my way to Wales to look for my father."

"Wales is a wild place," another voice responded. "I wouldn't go there. What is your father doing there?"

Should she tell them that he was on the run from the King's men? That was nothing to do with her, and villagers were not usually supporters of the King's emissaries, unless there was a price on someone's head.

"He is running from the King's men." There. It was out. Maybe it would distract them from thoughts of witches. "He helped a thief escape from London, and now they are after him." Another lie, but surely all concerned would forgive her.

There were some chuckles in the crowd. Either her story was humorous, or they didn't believe her.

As the laughter died away, an unearthly cackle arose from the woman tied to the stocks. "It's her familiar! I told you!"

Out of the corner of her eye, Brianna caught a glimpse of an orange cat streaking across the far corner of the town square. Orangino! But was he letting her know he was here? Or warning her? There was no way to know. But the distraction did seem to divert the attention of the men from interrogating Brianna.

"We have a witch to burn," the burly one who held Brianna arm stated.

Brianna thought her heart stopped, before it began pounding at a terrifying pace. Where they going to burn her? Had they already decided she was a witch?

But the man continued, never loosening his hold on her. Her arms were going to be bruised and sore, if she lived to feel it. "What is your father called?" he asked.

"Sir Michael." She hoped that the title would lend credence to her story. Even rough villagers on a witch hunt would have some respect for a knight of the realm, if only because they feared retribution if they harmed his daughter.

"I know of no Sir Michael," the man answered. The other villagers nodded their heads in agreement.

"Have you heard of every knight in the service of the king?" Brianna countered.

No one answered. Finally the man who still gripped Brianna's upper arm admitted, "No. We have not. But how do we know you are telling the truth?"

"How do you know I'm not?" Her strength grew as she felt their arguments tilting off balance. They had no real reason to hold her, if they had no evidence, however flimsy, that she was a witch. But she knew evidence of witchcraft was always flimsy because it played on the people's fears.

Even as she began to feel that they would not burn her for a witch, another fear took hold. They believed she was a boy. In her trousers and short hair, and in the dim torchlight, they had no reason to believe otherwise. The man who held her had only gripped her arm. But she knew she had to escape the village before they had cause to question her gender. She breathed deeply, calling on the glamour of magic to appear as a boy. As long as they did not inadvertently touch the soft parts of her body that would give her away, she might be able to pull it off.

Abruptly the man released her. "You'll stay for the witch burning." He nodded toward the old woman in her restraints. "Then you can be on your way." He gave Brianna a hard look while another man tossed her bag at her feet. Evidently they had found nothing within it that they thought suspicious. Anyone could carry herbs, and the large piece of cloth that she intended as a skirt could be anything, including a blanket.

The sky had turned a faint orange in the east. "Start piling the kindling. You, too," The man who had held her directed his gaze to Brianna. "The witch burns at first light."

Brianna had no desire to watch the woman burn. Witch burnings were not that uncommon in the villages of England, and even happened occasionally in the larger towns, but Brianna had never seen one. It was doubly repugnant to her because she knew that magic existed, it just was not the type of magic that people believed witches possessed, and that they feared. The real magic was no threat to the religion of the land or the king, or any of its people. It was simply a way of thinking, a way of using your own intelligence and inner power to do good. But what people did not understand, they feared. That much she had learned from Rowena.

But the woman in the stocks had called Brianna a witch! She would have the girl burn with her if she could! However, since the first outburst, the old woman had fallen silent. Brianna glanced at her as she reluctantly carried a load of sticks and dumped them at the bottom of the framework. The woman's head hung on her chest, and she seemed to sleep. Brianna quickly stood and returned for another load, being careful to blend in with the group of men and boys who were assembling, and not to call attention to herself. Least of all, to call the attention of the old woman. Could she tell that Brianna was not the boy she claimed to be? Women often could sense these things when men could not. Was the woman really a witch? Brianna doubted it. Women and men with real magical powers were too smart to get caught up in a net of witch hunters. They could certainly find themselves in other kinds of trouble, as Brianna well knew, but not a victim of witch burning, drowning, or whatever other punishments superstitious Englishmen dreamed up.

As she followed her instructions, walking back and forth with armloads of kindling with the others, she began to form a plan for escape. Once the fire was lit, the town would be suffused with excitement. All eyes would be on the poor woman who would suffer a most excruciating death by fire. Brianna would take that opportunity to slip out of the village and be on her way. By the time they realized she was gone, she would be well on her way in the direction of Wales. She had only to keep a low profile until then.

At last the sky was nearly light. The torches were extinguished, and old men, women and children emerged from their houses, rubbing sleep from their eyes, eager for the morning spectacle. Some shared hunks of bread. Just the sight of the food made Brianna's stomach grumble, and she wondered if she had anything left in her pack, or if those who searched it had taken her last bits of food. She opened the bag and fumbled around in the bottom, hoping against hope.

There was a small chunk of bread, apparently too dried out for even these poor folk. And something else. Her fingers closed on a small, hard object. Without removing her hand completely from the bag, she looked at the object. A dark stone, sharp on the edges. It felt like the gems from old King John's treasure that had turned up first in the village by the Wash, and then before she left Rowena's. It had not been there before. She knew it as a sign of protection.

Chapter 28

"Courage is like magic, courage vanishes crisis."

Amit Kalantri

Magic Realm

"She won't know what to do with it." Rhys, Brianna's magical grandmother spoke. "You have overwhelmed her. Our granddaughter is on the run in fear of her life, disguised as a boy, and you drop another of the king's jewels into her bag. You are distracting her from the task at hand, which is to escape this village of suspicious ignorant characters." The woman rose from her chair to look at the sky. Lincoln was relatively safe from German bombers in the World War II years, but planes from an Allied airfield nearby could often be seen. She watched them now, in the brightening dawn sky, as they returned from their missions. "Those poor boys," she whispered to herself, before returning to the discussion at hand. England in the 1940s and the 1200s were two totally different places in time, and Rhys was not sure which of them was the more frightening.

"Trust her." Rhys's husband Jonathan, Brianna's grandfather, spoke. "Being strong in your magic is more than knowing how to use spells and potions. She has to use her mind. She has to be able to think clearly in a crisis. She will be all right."

"I hope so." Rhys sighed, her eyes darting back and forth between the darkening sky and the castle room, warmed by a crackling fire. "But she won't get the strength from either

her mother or her father. Her mother is a scatterbrained, silly girl, even though she is past thirty now. And her father doesn't even know that he has magical powers, or that he is her father! From where will she draw her magic?"

"From herself," Jonathan crossed the room to stand next to his wife. "Just watch her." He laid his hand gently on Rhys's shoulder. Together they returned to the center of the room, to the fire that burned continually in the hearth. "Watch."

The flames crackled and spun into a whirl of flame in the grate, and dissolved into the scene miles away in the village of Swindon.

They watched as Brianna dropped the gem back into the bag. It had come there by magic, of that she had no doubt. She hoisted the bag onto her shoulders and took a place at the edge of the crowd. Pulling her cap down tightly over her now short curls, she hoped to blend into the crowd of villagers as much as possible. She cringed as the first torch was touched to the kindling surrounding the helpless woman, who still slumped in her bonds. Maybe she was already dead. Brianna hoped so. But no. She saw movement and the woman twitched in a violent spasm and then screamed. Brianna could take no more. While all eyes and ears were on the helpless victim, she slipped out of the square and ran along the side of the church toward the edge of the village. She saw the woods beyond and knew that the road west lay to the right. They would not bother to follow her for some time, if at all, but they knew she was headed toward Wales. She would do well to avoid the road if she could.

But now, she ran. As fast as her legs could carry her, Brianna ran down the road that led away from the village, where she could still hear the screams of the dying woman, and knew that the crowd's attention was riveted on the scene, their taste for blood and death being satisfied once again. But when the excitement had died down, someone would surely think to look for the young boy on his way to Wales. Brianna's lungs burned but she continued to run, the dim morning light helping her to avoid ruts in the road, which could cause her a twisted ankle if not worse. At last she could run no more and slowed to a walk. She risked turning to look over her shoulder. The sky was brightening in the east, and the flames from the village were still visible. No one seemed to be pursuing her, however. Certainly she would hear them if they were. She left the road and slipped into the trees and circled back around to the wood where her horse waited. Normally she slept during the day and traveled at night, but she wanted to put as much distance as possible between the last village and herself, and she was too keyed up to sleep right now. She looked around for her cat Orangino, but did not seen him. *He will turn up*, she thought. *He always does.*

She was about to mount Belle when a flash of orange told her Orangino had been waiting for her as well. He streaked through the underbrush and she followed, coming out onto a little used path that seemed to parallel that of the road out of the village. As she followed on horseback, she heard the sound of horse's hooves. It sounded like only one horse, and coming from the west, so not from the village. It was not someone on her trail. Brianna hid behind the trees and waited. A rider traveling at that speed was not interested in a young boy on the run from villagers. And sure enough, the rider passed her in an instant, heading toward the village. She watched him disappear into the rising sun, shading her eyes against the brightness. She had only been able to see that it was a large man, dressed in ordinary peasants clothing. He was not a knight. She had no way to know what his business could be to travel in such a hurry, but it had nothing to do with her. And perhaps whatever it was, it would distract the villagers from any thoughts of pursuing her. She shrugged and turned once again toward the west, keeping to the edge of the road now that it was daylight.

Chapter 29

"Trust thyself: every heart vibrates to that iron string."

Ralph Waldo Emerson, *Self-Reliance*

Michael woke from a deep sleep. For a moment he could not think where he was. But he was warm and relaxed, and felt rested. Soft voices murmured somewhere nearby, and he could smell fresh bread and maybe even meat. He moved his limbs and felt their strength. Wherever he was, everything seemed to be in good order. He was aware of someone standing next to him and rolled over to see a young girl of maybe seven years old, holding an earthenware mug of something fragrant and steamy. He sat up, pulling the bed clothes around his body and rubbing his hands across his face and through his hair. Something had happened yesterday, something good, but he couldn't remember what it was. He smiled at the girl, who stood patiently waiting for him to wake up, and finally accepted the mug from her hands. "Thank you."

She bobbed a small curtsey and hurried back across the room toward the sound of the other voices and the warmth of the fire. Michael sipped the hot liquid, which was some type of tea made from herbs, sweet and spicy at the same time. He became more aware of his surroundings and saw that the cottage, if that was what it was, was larger than those of most peasants, but there seemed to be only this one room. There were other platforms for sleeping on the same side of the room where he lay. He wondered how many people lived here. He counted four small children at a table near the fire, and two women seated near the fire, one occasionally stirring something in a pot that hung from a hook over the flames. Michael drained the cup and realized he needed to relieve himself soon. He found his trousers lying at the foot of his bed and reached to pull them on for modesty's sake. His movements caught the eye of the younger of the two women, who handed her wooden spoon to her companion and walked toward Michael with a smile. She was probably in her twenties, her dark blonde hair pulled back roughly into a knot at the back of her head. Her clothing was various shades of brown, as most peasants did not have access to colorful dyes that the lords and ladies of the court and the larger towns used. But she wore a dark blue ribbon around her neck, from which was suspended a tiny stone. As the light from the flames caught the facets of the stone, Michael knew that it was a diamond. Where did a peasant woman get a diamond?

"I see you are awake. And I am sure you need to go outside." She nodded toward the door. "It is almost light. You will find water in the trough just outside the door. It is clean and fresh."

Michael thanked her and quickly slipped out. As the woman had said, the water in the trough was clean and crystal clear, although icy cold. He wondered that there were not ice crystals still present, but perhaps he was not the first person to wash this morning. And it was morning, although barely. The sky to the east, down the mountain where this cottage was situated, was brightening as he watched. Any second the sun would rise above the horizon on what appeared to be a cloudless day.

As he watched the sun rise, his memory began to return. He was in Wales, or at least he thought he was. That was the last place he remembered, going to sleep in a cottage after riding on a hunt with the men who had seemed to be waiting for him. They had ridden for several hours and finally returned with only two rabbits. It had seemed less a hunt and more a ride to confuse their visitor. He had been exhausted when they returned and fell immediately into a deep sleep. And where was young Mory? A frisson of panic shot through Michael. These people spoke English, or at least the woman did. Now that he thought about it, the young girl who brought him the tea had said nothing, and he had not heard the voices of the others in the cottage well enough to determine what language they spoke. As he stood watching the sunrise, lost in his thoughts, he felt a soft touch on his left forearm, although he had heard no one approach.

The young woman who had spoken to him indoors smiled up at him. She had straight, even teeth, with none missing that he could see. Her skin still appeared creamy, no doubt due to the climate, although her eyes conveyed a sense of experience and perhaps trials in her life. "Come. No doubt you have questions. I think I can answer them for you." Her voice was melodious, but he could not determine the accent. She spoke English flawlessly. Still, he felt uneasy. Where was Mory?

She read his thoughts, or so it seemed. "You are worried about your young friend Mory."

"Yes. Where is he?"

"He is safe. We sent him to spend the night with young Robert. I only had room for one here."

Young Robert. He remembered something now.

"I need to find him," Michael said, clearing his throat and attempting to step away from the touch that was somehow disconcerting, but she held fast to his arm. When he looked at her, the rising sun caught the diamond at her throat and the sparkle nearly blinded him. The glow spread to her blue eyes, which shone like sapphires, and her smile possessed an unearthly quality. "Who are you?" he whispered, although he could hear no sound from his lips.

He sensed her words rather than heard them. "I am Mara, friend of Rowena. And others."

"You know Rowena?" he gasped. When he thought of the old woman, a strange sadness came over him. Had something happened to Rowena? And the young girl Brianna? And how did this woman on a mountaintop in Wales know about Rowena?

He stared at Mara. She held his gaze and her eyes seemed to laugh at him. "Come. Have something to eat. I'll send the children out to care for the sheep and we will talk." He wanted to refuse. He wanted to say, *I want answers now!* But he knew it was useless. A beautiful woman always had the power to sway him, and this was more than a beautiful woman such as he had seen in the courts of kings. This was a woman whose beauty was in her inner power. *No man has such power*, he thought.

His breakfast was simple but filling: a couple of slices of cold mutton along with fresh cheese and bread, and ale to wash it down. He knew everything came from the hands of the woman who served the food to him, and from the land around them. What a beautiful life they had here! Maybe this was what he should strive for. Life on a mountain top with a beautiful woman. It would be a simple life, much better than chasing around the country in the service of a king who cared nothing for the fate of his knights, and truthfully did not even know of their existence as individuals. Finally the children were sent out to care for the sheep and Mara sat down on the chair across from him. "You want answers," she said simply. "I will give them to you."

"Who are you?" he blurted out, realizing at once that he should wait for her to speak, since she was obviously ready to do so.

She smiled. "My name is Mara. I told you that."

"Yes." He shifted on his seat. It wasn't a physical discomfort he felt, but something more, something deeper.

He felt as if his spirit were struggling to understand something, something just beyond the grasp of his all too human mind. "And you are a friend of Rowena's." Again that sense of fear shot through him. "How do you know Rowena?"

"Rowena is my mother. But our connection is more than mother and daughter, as mortals understand it."

"Mortals?" he asked. "What are you saying? I know there are some who believe that Rowena has magical powers, but . . ."

"And you don't?" Her words were challenging, but her blue eyes sparkled with laughter, and a smile crinkled the corners of her mouth.

"I . . ." He cleared his throat. "I don't know. There is something . . ." He sighed and looked into Mara's eyes and felt himself sinking. He thought at first that he was falling, perhaps he was not as strong as he thought, or perhaps she had put something in the food. But no. He still sat on the wooden bench; his hands still rested on the table. "What's going on?"

"Don't try so hard." Her voice seemed to come from far away, or all around, or maybe somewhere inside him. It was impossible to tell.

He tried to pull himself back to reality, at least the reality he knew. "Just tell me if Rowena and the girl Brianna are all right."

"You are worried about them?"

"Yes. I am. I should never have left. Soldiers in Worcester were bound to discover the whereabouts of the girl, and then both of them would be in danger. Trial for witchcraft is not a pretty sight."

"I know," she said, in a voice that forced him to blink his eyes. Of course she knew. She was a witch as well. "They are safe."

"I was afraid . . ."

"You spend too much time being afraid. That is one thing you need to eliminate from your life. You also need to listen. You did not allow me to finish."

"I'm sorry." He shifted again on his seat. He wanted to stand and pace around the room, but felt that Mara would not approve. Now he needed the approval of this woman he barely knew. What was going on?

Mara looked at him again with those knowing eyes, eyes that glowed of their own power. Power. That was what she had. No man on earth had the power he sensed in this woman. "You are about to take on a new role, Michael who calls himself Sir Michael." The slight smile played around her lips again. "Your daughter needs you, Michael. You must find her and bring her here."

If there was anything Michael was expecting, it wasn't that. Sure he had had relationships with women, but he was not a father. Or was he? He swallowed hard. "Who is my daughter, and where is she?"

"The girl Brianna is your daughter," she answered softly as she touched his hand with a gentleness that sent tingles from his head to his toes.

"Brianna?" He cleared his throat and repeated her name. "Brianna? You said she was safe."

A gentle smile creased Mara's face again. "You aren't shocked that she is your daughter, but only think of her safety. I think you've known since you met her in Newark that she was your flesh and blood."

Michael gulped and set down his mug of ale before he spilled it. "And Rowena?"

"Rowena has traveled to the next world. She was an old woman and it was time."

"You said she was safe, too! What else aren't you telling me?" He stood too quickly, knocking over the wooden chair and sending it clattering to the floor. The old dog snoozing by the fire raised his head, but seeing his mistress with her usual calm demeanor, he lowered it and returned to sleep.

"Rowena is safe now in the next world. Nothing can harm her. I am in communication with her and the rest of the magic world."

"That's great for you!" he shouted, and the dog raised his head again. "That's great for you," he repeated in a quieter tone. "You tell me Rowena is dead, and Brianna is my daughter and needs my help, but she is safe. How am I supposed to help her? Where is she?"

"There is more that you need to know." Mara placed her hand on his forearm, feeling the tension in his muscles. "Sit, Michael. You need to listen. I know knights are not trained to listen, except to execute orders, but you are more than a knight."

He sat. "All right. Tell me what I need to know so I can go find Brianna."

That smile again, crinkling her lips. "I can see why you became such a brave knight. Such determination. But yes. I will tell you." She closed her eyes for a moment and breathed deeply. "You are more than a knight, Michael. That is why your relationship with Brianna's mother, whose name is Marged, by the way, produced the child Brianna, a girl with extraordinary magical powers. Unfortunately, your relationship was doomed. Marged rejected her powers. Consequently, she never trained Brianna properly. Through your help, Brianna found her way to Rowena, who provided the magical education that Brianna needed. Her training is nearly complete. Her powers are strong. But then Rowena died."

"Marged." Michael whispered the name. He remembered her. Of course he did. That was why he felt that he had seen Brianna before. It was the resemblance to her mother, and maybe also a fleeting resemblance to himself. It had been long ago, nearly fourteen years. Marged had been a beautiful, mercurial woman, little more than a girl. He met her in a small village near the Wash where she lived with a man and woman who he thought were her parents. She had seemed restless, and this quality had frightened him. He was not ready for marriage, and he sensed that she was trouble. After a brief romance, and some stolen nights under the stars, he left her. He had no idea that she carried his child. Suddenly a torrent of doubt coursed through him. "How do I know you are telling the truth?"

"Why would I lie?" Mara's voice was like silk.

"Maybe you are Marged's sister or friend, or have some other reason of your own to send me on a wild goose chase for Brianna. Maybe you think that telling me she is my daughter will entice me to go on a quest that could lead me into a trap or get me killed."

"You want proof." Mara smoothed her long sleeves with her slim hands.

"Yes. I need something."

Very well. I will show you who you are. Once you know who you are, you will recognize who Marged and Brianna are, and you will know what you have to do." She stood and extended her hand to him.

He rose and joined her as she led him to the fire that burned in the hearth. The flames had subsided after the morning's cooking, but as the two approached, Mara released Michael's hand and extended both of her own to the flames, which rose before swirling into a ball of fire that moved to hover in front of them. "Don't be afraid. Reach out your hands and take the fire. This is not mortal fire. This fire will show you who you are."

Fearlessly, for he was a knight, Michael extended his hands to the ball of flame which seemed to settle in his palms. Mara was right. He felt no burning, just a warmth that suffused his body. And then he was no longer standing in front of the fire. He was back in the village with Marged, listening to her laughter, succumbing to her touch. Like magic, he had told her, not knowing that he spoke the truth. And the couple with whom she lived. They were not her parents. Just as he accepted that knowledge, he was somewhere else. A castle. He was a boy again with his parents, before disease had struck their town and his family decimated, before he was taken into training for knighthood by Sir Alfred. Tears filled his eyes as he remembered that long ago time. He had almost forgotten his parents. A knight of the king had no time to dwell on such sentimental thoughts. He reached out his hand to his mother and father, who smiled and extended their hands to him. He knew this wasn't real, that Mara's magic had caused him to remember his childhood and his mother and father, so he was amazed when he felt the physical sensation of their flesh and blood hands. The jolt of their touch made him cry out as they gathered him to their bodies. He did not remember that such love existed. But more than their love, he felt an electricity course through him, and he remembered now. He remembered. "You will go on without us, dear Michael. We cannot stay. Do not forget us, and do not forget that we pass the magic to you."

And he was back in the cottage with Mara. The ball of fire was gone from his hands, back in its rightful place in the hearth. But he remembered now. He also possessed magic.

Mara's smile was full of kindness and compassion. "Your mother and father wait in the next world, and you will see them again. But now that you remember who you are, and the powers you possess, you have a job to do." She took his hand and led him back to the table. "Sit. You have a grueling trek before you. You need to rest as much as possible."

When they were seated across from each other, Mara took each of his hands in her own. "You and Marged created a beautiful child named Brianna, a child with the magic of both her parents. Strong magic. She has now received some training from the witch Rowena, who has joined your parents in the next world. Brianna is on her way to Wales, because she knows this is where you were headed, where you would be safe from the English."

"Is she in danger?" Now that he knew that Brianna was his daughter, he felt a worry for her that surpassed anything he had felt before. He had cared for her before, before he knew of their relationship. Now his concern was overwhelming. If anything should happen to her, now that he knew that she was his daughter, he felt he could not survive.

"Not immediately," Mara answered. "She has your strength and common sense. She has escaped a village where the townspeople were in the process of burning a witch. Poor woman. But her pain is past now." She was silent for a moment, as they both pondered the painful death the woman had suffered. "Brianna is traveling dressed as a boy, which is protecting her somewhat."

"Where is she?" Michael asked.

"She isn't far from the Marches, the border territory between England and Wales. Perhaps a day's walk. But it is risky territory, and she is a girl alone. Even a young boy traveling alone is not entirely safe, and her disguise may not protect her."

Michael nodded, thinking of the dangers his daughter would be facing on the road. "I don't know any magic," he said suddenly.

"It will come to you," Mara answered. "The powers that watch over you both will see that you have the magic you need at the time you need it. And remember that Brianna is well-trained. Between the two of you, you will protect each other."

"Come." Mara stood and took Michael's hand. "You have no time to lose. I must create the magic that will take you to Brianna, because it would take days for you to walk there."

"I have one question." When Michael stood, he towered above Mara, who had seemed taller when they spoke earlier.

"What is your question?"

"Where is Marged?"

"Marged." Mara's eyes focused into the distance beyond the cottage, where the green Welsh hills faded into blue in the distance. "Marged is untrained, unwilling to learn, and therefore dangerous. She has been sent forward into the future, far into the future, where she can do no harm. Once Brianna is safe, Marged will return to our time." She lowered her eyes. "There are other things that have been sent forward in time so that they will do no harm. You remember old King John's treasure that was lost in the Wash?"

"Of course. The servants in charge would have been severely punished if the king had not conveniently died a week later. I thought there was something strange at the time, but I suspected some of the nobles who were owed money spirited it off for their own purposes."

"Funny you should use the word 'spirited," Mara said as they walked toward the door, "because that is what happened. The treasure was spirited away into the magic world."

They had reached the door, and Michael was about to ask another question, but Mara stopped him with a finger to his lips. The sun was high in the sky, turning the hills to gold. "You must go. Your horse is ready."

"But . . ." Michael still had no idea how he was going to travel from the Brecon Beacons to the English side of the Marches.

Mara placed two fingers between her lips and whistled. A black horse, saddled and ready, bounded from the stable. "You will find everything you need in the saddlebags. Now." She pointed to a woods of trees a slight way down the hill to the east. "With your love for your daughter in your heart, ride through those trees. When I see you next you will be together."

Michael mounted and took the reins in his hands. He turned to look at Mara. "But how will I . . .?"

"You will." Mara slapped the flank of the horse and they were gone.

Chapter 30

"Being deeply loved by someone gives you strength, while loving someone deeply gives you courage."

Lao Tzu

Michael slowed the horse as they entered the woods. He normally did not like riding through dark forested areas; there was too much danger of highwaymen lying in wait where they could not be seen, but he did not feel that sense of foreboding here. He was only a few hundred yards from Mara's cottage, and he kept his thoughts on Brianna. The road bore to the left and he followed it, finding himself on a stretch that was straight toward the east, toward England. Or maybe it was England. There was something about the orderliness of the hedges and the straightness of the road that made him think that he was in England. As simple as that, he was in England. He peered into the darkness that was already settling on the land, and distinguished a small figure approaching him on horseback.

He knew at once that it was Brianna. Should he wait for her or approach? Better to wait. She might become frightened if he approached her. *Use your magic*, Mara had said. He closed his eyes and visualized Brianna on the road, and then saw, in his mind's eyes, the two of them riding together to Wales. He could not see farther than that. He opened his eyes and felt the tug of energy between them. She was closer. He knew she could see him. Did she recognize him? She continued at the same steady pace, riding at the very edge of the road, where she would be less visible than if she traveled in the center. There was a rustle in the grass, and an orange cat bounded out onto the road in front of her. He remembered that cat -- Orangino. Wasn't that what she called it? That boy Thomas who accused her of witchcraft had called it her familiar. Maybe it was.

Closer now, he could see that she was smiling. "Sir Michael," she called. "Are you waiting for me?"

"I've come to take you to Wales."

"Thank you."

As she stopped speaking her horse whinnied, and the cat Orangino growled fiercely and leapt into Brianna's arms.

"What . . .?" she began. And then they heard the hooves of many horses pounding in the distance from the east, and coming closer. "From the village! I thought I had escaped them!"

"Follow me!" He turned his horse back toward the way he had come, toward Wales. Just then Orangino leapt to the ground and into the undergrowth at the side of the road. Michael looked disconcerted for a moment, but this time Brianna reassured him.

"He can take care of himself. He is a magical cat."

Without another word, he turned his mount around and urged him into a gallop toward the west. They rode hard until Michael could tell that the horses were growing tired and he slowed to a walk. They could still hear the riders behind them, but they had not gained on them. "We can't risk going into a village," he said softly. "It's dark now."

"I always rode through the night," Brianna answered.

"You are a brave girl, much braver than any girl I've known."

She said nothing.

"We can't ride through the night. There is too much risk that we will be heard, and someone will become suspicious, or report hearing us. We need a place to hide."

The deepening darkness made it nearly impossible to see beyond the road, and clouds were gathering, making the chances of moonlight less likely. As they peered into the night, they heard a meow a few yards off the road to the left, and could just discern glowing orange eyes peering at them. "Orangino," Brianna whispered. "Follow him."

Michael pulled on the reins to turn his horse off the road. The stallion seemed to know that the small orange beast was leading him to rest and safety, if not food, and followed willingly. The ground was rough but not treacherous, and in a few moments they reached the cover of dense trees. Orangino had disappeared. Michael continued riding slowly, allowing his mount to carefully set one hoof in front of the other, as it was nearly impossible to see where they were going. A fat raindrop landed on Brianna's nose, causing her to jump. She hoped they reached shelter soon or they would be drenched, and the temperature was dropping as darkness fell.

They were almost upon their shelter before they realized it, and would have fallen over a cliff if Orangino's glowing eyes had not alerted them to the direction they should travel. A path wound down toward a small stream, and the cat turned at their approach and strode down the path, tail held high.

"I think we should walk," Michael pulled his horse to a stop. "Can you make it?"

"Oh, yes." Brianna jumped nimbly to the ground. It was not yet wet enough to slip on the leaves and mud that would surely cover the ground in a few moments. Michael followed her, as they lead their mounts slowly down the path after the orange cat.

The cave was small but large enough for the horse to step inside out of the rain, which was coming down harder. "They won't pursue us in this," Michael commented. "But still it is better to be as quiet as possible."

Brianna nodded, her eyes wide. Now that they had reached some safety, her mind was beginning to work. How had he found her? What did he know about her? Where -- besides to Wales -- was he taking her? She looked for Orangino, always her barometer of the safety of a situation. The cat sat in the farthest, driest corner of the cave, serenely licking his paws, which had undoubtedly become soiled by mud on the walk down to the cave. They were safe, at least for now.

Michael was caring for the horses, rubbing their coats dry before small bags of oats that he fastened to each as a nosebag. The horses ate eagerly, crunching the grain with satisfaction. "No one can hear them in this rain," Michael whispered. Their eyes had by now adjusted to the near darkness, and Brianna could just see the outline of the large black horse with its rider standing next to it. "This rain will last for a while," he said. "Why don't you sleep? I'll stand guard. We are safe enough." As if to confirm his words, a flash of lightening illuminated the entrance to the cave, showing nothing but blackness beyond.

Brianna wondered how she could possibly sleep. She was cold and uneasy. She should feel much more secure with both Michael and Orangino keeping watch, but she was still keyed up after what she knew was a narrow escape from the village. Any village that will burn a suspected witch would have no qualms about accusing a girl traveling alone and disguised as a boy. And they would have discovered her secret, of that she had no doubt. If they did not immediately kill her, she had no doubt the men of the village would have had their way with her first.

But she did sleep, although it was a troubled rest with the rain and wind outside the cave. She dreamt that she was in a dungeon deep in the earth. She could smell the damp earthiness and struggled to wake herself, but exhaustion pulled her back, kept her locked in the dungeon until the dreams left some hours later and she rested, an orange cat curled close by her side.

Then she heard her name. "Brianna. Brianna, you have to wake up." She turned her aching body, disturbing Orangino who sat up to study their surroundings. "Brianna, we have to get out of the cave now." She could hear the water and the wind. It did not seem to her a good time to travel. But she looked at the worried face above her. Sir Michael. He had come for her and brought her here to this hideout.

"What?" She raised herself on a elbow, trying to clear her head.

"The water is rising. The cave will be flooded soon. We have to get out now." Dizzily she made it to her feet. "Come. I'll help you onto your horse."

"I have to . . ." She looked around the cave. Her bladder was full and the sound of the rain wasn't helping the feeling.

"We've got to get out of the cave first. The river could pour in here at any moment." He picked up her bag and Orangino leapt toward it, settling himself in it depths. Even he knew that they had to leave.

"All right." She put out her arms for the bag and settled it across her shoulders, accepting Michael's assistance in mounting the horse. As soon as she was settled, he swung himself into his own saddle on the horse in front of her and urged him forward out of the cave. Brianna saw immediately that his urgency had not been misplaced. The swollen river was already lapping at the banks. A surge from upstream would send water into the cave. They could have been drowned, or at the least trapped in a sodden refuge. The horse hesitated, but Sir Michael's gentle voice urged the animal up the slope to high ground with sure hooves. Brianna hugged her shawl around her but it did little to keep her dry. Orangino rested in his nest in front of her, so the cat would be relatively dry, but he was the only one.

Lightning flashed in the distance, followed by a crack of thunder. The storm seemed to be moving away, but the rain still pounded and the wind had not abated. They reached the road and Michael turned his horse westward toward Wales, but they were still a long way from safety.

Chapter 31

"A ship in harbor is safe, but that is not what ships are built
for."
John A. Shedd

At this point Brianna cared little for safety. She just
wanted to be dry and warm. She and Michael had continued
to ride in the pouring rain for what seemed like hours,
although there was no way to tell how much time had passed.
The sky was still just as dark. It could be morning. It could
be noon. She wondered how anyone, soldiers or irate
villagers, could be chasing them in this weather. Brianna
could not remember ever feeling so miserable. She amused
herself -- if you could call it amusement -- by thinking of
times in her life when she had felt miserable and comparing
them to her present situation. There was the time when she
and her mother were caught in the rain when they were out
collecting herbs in the woods near their village. They had
been wet, but not so cold as this, and they were no more than
a fifteen-minute walk from home, a warm fire and dry
clothes. And there was the time when she and the witch
Rowena ran out of firewood. But that had been for no more
than a few hours, until a kind villager had restocked their
supply. No, nothing was worse than the present situation.
She had been in danger for her life in the past, too. But never
all this misery at once.

Finally, Michael turned his horse off the soggy road and
rode into a thicket of trees just off the trail. The low-hanging
branches offered some protection, and although they were
still wet and cold, at least there was some respite from the

driving rain. "I just want to let the horses rest a few moments." Michael dismounted and rummaged in a saddlebag for oats and nosebags for the horses, who accepted the food with a satisfied whinnies. Then he handed Brianna some oat bread and a hunk of cheese, miraculously dry.

"Thank you," she whispered and she began to chew. She hadn't realized how hungry she was. She had been so busy being cold and wet.

Sir Michael tucked into his own breakfast. After a few moments of quiet eating, Brianna asked, "Are we safe now?"

He laughed. "Safer than we were. We are not in a cave that is probably flooded by now. And it is doubtful anyone is near to catching up with us in this weather. We are a few miles closer to Wales and safety."

"Why is Wales safer than England?" Brianna shivered with cold. Now that her hunger was somewhat satisfied, her awareness of the cold and wet returned.

Michael laughed again, a musical chuckle that sent a shiver of happiness up her spine and took her by surprise. If she had to be in this wretched situation, she was glad that Sir Michael was with her. She knew he would do anything in his power to keep her safe. She had never even felt that way even with her mother. Her mother had expected more of her little girl. She had treated her as an equal, which was wonderful in some senses, but sometimes it was important just to feel safe and cared for.

"English law does not reach into Wales," he answered. "At least not beyond the Marches, and not much even there. Once you reach the Brecon Beacons, there is no danger from the English, soldiers or otherwise. The language is different. I've learned a little of it, but only because I had help. The mountains are rugged and dangerous. The Welsh are a determined people who protect what is theirs and those they wish to protect." He looked up into the trees, where it seemed the rain has diminished ever so slightly. "The sooner we reach the Marches, the better off we will be."

"Are we close?" Brianna shivered again, but from cold this time.

"I'm not sure in this rain." Michael studied Brianna and looked again at the sky. "We need to get you into something dry. I don't want to bring you all this way and have you sicken."

"You have something dry?" This was more than she had dared hope for. As much as she enjoyed their stop, she knew they would be moving on, back into the rain, very soon.

He opened the saddlebag again and pulled out a rough wool blanket. "It may itch a bit, but it's dry and warm. The rain has abated enough that you won't be soaked through." He helped her removed her own sodden cloak and settle the blanket around her shoulders, after rubbing her back and shoulders briskly with the rough blanket. He twisted her cloak and wrung out the water before stuffing it into his bag. "We'll get dried out soon enough. No rain lasts forever."

"What about you?" Brianna accepted his help to remount her horse.

"I'll be fine. I've been in worse."

Orangino had disappeared briefly into the undergrowth, but reappeared when he heard his mistress settled again on horseback. He wriggled his rear end and jumped deftly to the back of the horse into his spot in front of Brianna. His fur was damp, but his warm body was a comfort. Michael mounted Jupiter and guided him back to the road, where the rain had nearly stopped. He looked around; still no one on the road from either direction. They turned west and were soon in sight of a few houses. No one was out in the aftermath of the storm, but soon people would begin to emerge, and it would not do for them to report two riders on horseback, headed west.

Brianna dozed as she rode. She was only slightly less cold and wet, but enough to feel more relaxed. She awoke when she felt them slow and the horses turned once again off the road. When she opened her eyes, she saw a rough wooden shack in front of them. "Where are we?"

"I was told I would find this shack." Michael sounded pleased.

"What is special about it?" Brianna yawned, still unsure of her surroundings.

"Look." He pointed to the roof, where some symbols Brianna did not recognize were carved into the worn wood. Or did she recognize them? The star was identical to the tattoo on her arm.

Chapter 32

"Life is a series of natural and spontaneous changes. Don't resist them; that only creates sorrow. Let reality be reality. Let things flow naturally forward in whatever way they like."

Lao Tzu

"They are safe," Jonathan, the master wizard, was looking into the fire where he watched Brianna and Michael enter the cabin. "Michael was drawn to the spell we cast on the cabin. He is about to accept his own magic." The old wizard chuckled. "I hate to see a human in such confusion, and Michael has become more and more confused. But now I think he has recovered from the shock of learning that Brianna is his daughter."

Andera touched her father's arm as she, too, stared into the flames. "It worries me, father."

"Oh, why?"

"How will Marged feel? She doesn't know anything about this. She has probably forgotten Michael's name. And in spite of all her faults, she is Brianna's mother."

Jonathan turned to his older daughter. "Marged is an adult. It's time for her to grow up. She needs to take responsibility for her life. Right now she is flitting around with soldiers from over 700 years in the future. At least she can't leave Dover Castle. And the soldiers will only remember her as a dream -- or a ghost." He smiled into the fire. "No, I have to think of Brianna. She is the priority. She has strong magic, and so does her father. They both need to know that."

"And once they get to Wales, then what?" Jonathan's wife Rhys, the mother of Marged and Andera, spoke from a corner of the room where she had been knitting with a bright translucent wool. She set her work down on her chair and came over to the other three. Rhys had a slight limp, a result of a fall from a horse when she was a small child. "What are you thinking, Jonathan?" She laid her hand on his arm. He looked down lovingly into her blue eyes.

"I'm thinking that Wales will be the perfect place for both our granddaughter and her father to learn who they are, and what they are. The knowledge will strengthen them. When Marged returns, they will understand her, and know how to relate to her."

"They still have a long way to go," Andera interjected. "They've barely reached the Marches."

"Maybe we can give them a little help." Jonathan smiled. "After all, I am a wizard. And there isn't anything for them to learn by trudging through the Marches and up into the Brecan Beacons on their own."

The old wizard held out his hands toward his wife. She reached into the air above her head and with one hand plucked down a feathered wand. With the other, she retrieved from the ether a handful of stars. She gave him the wand, and held the twinkling stars tightly cupped between her two hands. Their sparkling light, multi-colored in shades of purple, orange, green and red, pulsed between her palms. It seeped out between her fingers and turned them translucent. Jonathan held his wand above his head and muttered a few words before he dipped it into the handful of stars. He swirled the wand, catching up the stars like cotton candy and then plunged it into the flames in the hearth. The flames rose through the chimney, stars sparkling brightly, and were gone.

"There. Brianna and her father will awaken in the cottage of our Welsh witch. They will have knowledge that something has occurred, and they will believe. She will teach them what they need to know."

*****

The portal was open. Marged knew the opening between the worlds was in constant use by whoever was sent from the magical world to check on her, although she never saw them. She didn't even know if it was the same person each time, nor did she know where the portal was located -- until now. She had been walking around the lonely corridors of Dover Castle, amusing herself by trying to get lost, but it wasn't possible. The castle was built for convenience, and she had a magic sense of direction. She had just turned a corner when she tripped on the uneven floor. Instinctively her left hand went out to brace herself, when the wooden door to her left seemed to dissolve and her arm disappeared up to her elbow. Marged quickly pulled it back and stood staring at the door. It looked solid, like any other door in any other castle, but now she knew it wasn't. She also knew that her accidental touch had disturbed the magic realm, sending a shock wave throughout the atmosphere. But it was so quick that it might not have been noticed. Non-magical humans bumped into portals all the time, and while they might be noted, they were treated as isolated occurrences if they weren't repeated. They never were. Anyone who pushed their hand through a door into empty space would not be eager to try it again.

But it was Dover Castle, and Marged knew she was watched. Maybe she could escape if she moved quickly. Even if they recaptured her, it would be a break from this boring place. The giant metal birds from the twentieth century world vibrated overhead. They made Marged nervous. Now was the time to go. She had no idea where she would end up, but it didn't matter. Once she was free, she could find her way around and have some fun before they caught up with her. "They" meant her parents; she was still a child to them. Before she could think any farther, she pushed the portal and followed her hand through into darkness.

Marged loved the woosh through the darkness of the portal. Her skin tingled all over as if she were being rubbed by tiny stars. She opened her eyes wide, but could see nothing but blackness. Before she had always known where she was going. But this time when she passed through the portal in Dover, she left the twentieth century, but she never had a great sense of direction, and lacked the ability to concentrate for very long. She relaxed and was unprepared for the bump when she landed in a small dark room. She could hear voices, and recognized her mother's and that of her sister Andera. So she was home. That might be good and it might be bad. But somehow she had landed in a closet or storage room. She couldn't remember any such place in their home in Lincoln Castle. She took a step and stubbed her toe on a large bag that contained something hard and sharp. Curious, Marged bent and opened the drawstrings at the top of the bag. It felt like stones of various sizes, and something else. Marged closed her eyes and drew on her magical powers to project light into the bag. Gems! And -- gold! Had she stumbled on some magical treasure? Why had she never known about this? She must have made too much noise, or cast too much light, or maybe her mere presence had caused some shift in the magical atmosphere, because suddenly the door to the room was flung open, and Rhys and Andera stood above her, watching her running the rubies, diamonds, and emeralds through her fingers like pebbles on the beach.

"Marged, put those down and come out here this minute," her mother commanded.

Marged bristled. Did her mother think she was a child, talking to her like that? She stood, but both her mother and her sister were taller and she was still forced to look up at them. "What are those jewels doing here, and why was I never told about them?" she asked in her best voice of indignation.

"Come on out, "Rhys instructed her younger daughter. "I'll tell you about the jewels."

Marged wanted to argue and let her mother know what she thought about the way her family treated her, but she didn't. She followed her docilely to the main room where a fire crackled on the hearth.

"Sit down." Rhys's voice had the authority of someone used to giving orders. Marged sat. Andera walked around the room, making it clear that the order to sit was not for her. "Andera," her mother added. "Fetch us some wine. Warm, if you please."

Andera muttered a soft incantation before reaching her arms above her head. When she lowered them, she held a silver tray containing three steaming mugs of mulled wine. She set them on a small rough wooden table in from of her mother and sat next to her sister on the bench facing her. Rhys had taken the large chair where her husband normally sat.

The older woman held her mug between her two hands too warm them, but her eyes never left her daughter Marged's face. "How did you find the portal?"

"By accident. I was exploring the castle and just happened to put my hand out, and there it was."

"I see." Rhys sipped the hot wine and blew gently on its surface. "And you wanted to come home?"

"Yes." Marged began to cry, tears creating trails down her cheeks. She started to raise a corner of her skirt to wipe them away, but thought better of it. She didn't need a reprimand on manners on top of the other reprimands she was bound to receive.

Rhys handed her daughter a handkerchief. "Wipe your eyes, daughter."

Marged obeyed and blew her nose. Both her mother and her sister watched her. "And the jewels? That's what this is really all about, isn't it?"

Andera glanced at her mother, who nodded slightly, but Marged caught the signal. They had been doing that since her childhood, which was one of the reasons she ran away in the first place, before she met Michael, before Brianna was born.

"There is no reason she shouldn't know," Rhys said. "The curse on them is powerful."

Marged wondered why that was important, but before she could ask, Andera spoke. "The jewels are King John's treasure, that most of England believes were lost in the Wash."

"I've heard of that. It happened not long after I left the village, right before the king died. You took them?" Marged set down her nearly empty mug with a clunk.

"Yes, we took them." Marged had not seen her father enter the room, but then, she usually didn't. "But not for ourselves, of course. We in the magic world have no use for gold and jewels."

Andera handed a mug of hot wine to her father. He smiled his thanks to her and took a sip. "But those treasures didn't belong to King John, and if he lived, chances are he would have sold them to pay his debts. Or his nobles would have stolen them.

"So it was easy enough, with the king on his way to Newark, to mire the wagon carrying the jewels in the mud as it attempted to cross the narrow strip of the Wash. I tipped the wagon, and as I did so, I gathered the treasure into the world of magic."

Marged sat wide-eyed. She never knew her father had that much power. "And now what? Are you ever going to give it back?"

Jonathan looked uncomfortable, or as uncomfortable as a master magician could appear. "I hope so, but the way the future is looking, it will be in the far distant future in mortal time."

"After that terrible war I saw? With those metal birds in the sky, and those sweet soldiers I saw at the castle?" Her parents and sister exchanged looks again.

"Definitely not until after that." Marged's mother spoke softly, her voice filled with sorrow. "But the time will come when the English people, in fact all people, will realize that there are more important things in the world than gold, jewels and treasure. When they realize that they don't need those things anymore, the jewels will be returned."

Marged gaped at him. "They will get the jewels back when they don't need them anymore? That doesn't make any sense."

"Oh, but it makes perfect sense," her father answered. "You cannot possess anything, Marged. If you try to, it will only end up possessing you."

There was a whoosh in the chimney. The flames rose high and then subsided. Marged knew what that meant. Someone in another location in the magic world was contacting them. Her parents and Andera looked at each other, and then at Marged. "I know. I know. Why don't I go back to Dover Castle and the twentieth century for a while? I know you don't want me around when you talk with whoever wants to talk with you." She stood with a pout that she made sure both her parents and her sister observed.

"Promise you will stay out of trouble," her mother said.

"I will. I'll just check on my soldiers. I worry about them, you know."

"They won't even be born for more than seven hundred years," Andera commented with a knowing look of superiority at her sister.

Before either of the sisters could say anymore, their mother interrupted. "You know where the portal is. Be back in an hour, human time. If we want you sooner or want you to stay away longer, someone will come for you. If you disobey . . . ." Her words hung in the air.

"I know, mother." Marged rolled her eyes before turning toward the storage closet where she had emerged when she arrived.

"No!" Her mother shouted. "Don't go that way. Use the usual portal in the corridor. And go to Dover Castle, 1944. That's all."

Marged left the room. She was tempted to stand outside the door and listen, but changed her mind. They would catch her and there would be more trouble. She fingered the jewels in the pocket of her skirt and smiled to herself. Even powerful magicians like her parents and her sister had not detected what she had stolen after she arrived in the closet and found the treasure. And she knew just what she would do with them.

She sailed through the black space of time and emerged behind the door in the old castle. It was so similar to Lincoln Castle in some ways, but it smelled different. It was a different time, and on top of the dampness of stone and earth was layered something else. It was the smell of fire. But not the clean scent of a wood or peat fire. It was different, almost a metallic smell. It made her stomach feel queasy. She wondered how those young soldiers felt about it, or did they even notice it? Were they used to it? Was this how the twentieth century smelled?

Marged pushed open the door. The corridor was dark and quiet, but she could see flashes of light outside and hear the screams of the metal birds. What an unpleasant world this would be in the future! She glided along the passageway to an outside door and stepped out onto the ramparts. Ahead and down at ground level she could see the soldiers. Her soldiers. She hoped she didn't frighten them too much. She stayed close to the walls as she made her way to the entrance to the underground chambers where the soldiers did their work. There they were. Two stood at attention, guarding the entrance. Sentries were always the same, in whatever century. They tended to be among the youngest soldiers, standing with the weapons of their century, ready to defend their headquarters and their companions, but barely hiding the fear that they would actually need to act.

She eased herself through the gloomy night until she was just behind the taller of the two sentries. He was talking to his companion about his girl, and how they were planning to marry when the war was over, but he couldn't afford to buy a ring for her. Marged smiled. He would be able to give her a ring and more with what she was about to give him. Silently she inhaled and then exhaled, focusing on making herself as invisible as possible. It was not possible to be completely invisible. Only someone with her father's power could do that, but she would only be a presence to the young soldier, and he might and might not connect the presence of a ruby in his pocket with the ghostly woman who haunted Dover Castle. She stood so close to his back, that he must be able to feel her presence. He shivered. She slipped her hand into his right jacket pocket and left the ruby. Then she shrunk back against the stone.

"It's cold out here," he said. "Don't know where that cold draft comes from. I felt it a few days ago, and I just felt it again on my back."

"I haven't felt anything," his companion answered. "Must be a ghost," he added with a laugh.

Marged smiled mischievously. She had time for a bit of fun, and an emerald in her hand. She moved soundlessly behind the second soldier and placed her ephemeral body against his back, molding herself to him. She reached her arms around his chest and quickly slipped the emerald into his breast pocket. She hugged him tight before disappearing into the doorway to watch.

He stumbled. "Something just grabbed me. Did you see anything?" There was panic in his voice.

"No. Do you feel cold?"

"I'm freezing. Maybe the weather is changing." He stamped his feet and shook his head.

Marged covered her mouth with her hand to keep from giggling. He looked like a horse, stamping and shaking his head.

"Straighten up, Bill," the first soldier said. "It's time to do our rounds."

Marged froze in her place. If it was time to do their rounds, it was almost time for her to return to Lincoln and the thirteenth century. She pushed between them, nearly knocking the two of them off their feet, and ran to the other side of the castle and the portal. She glanced back once to see the two sentries staring after her. One had dropped his weapon on the ground. Their mouths hung open in shock. "Goodbye," she called.

She flew through the portal and arrived in Lincoln Castle gasping for breath and laughing.

"What trouble have you been causing, daughter?" her father asked. "I know you have done something. I know that laugh."

"We don't have time for that now, Jonathan." Marged's mother was walking around nervously, and Andera was nowhere to be seen.

"Why? What's up?" Marged asked.

"What's up?" her father repeated.

"That's something the soldiers say in the twentieth century," she answered with pride in her voice.

"You aren't in the twentieth century," he growled. "And you won't go back there if I have anything to say about it."

Marged started to counter with a retort but her mother stopped her with a hand on her arm. "We have no time for argument now. Marged, your daughter and her father will be arriving her in a few moments."

Chapter 33

"At the end of the day, it isn't where I came from. Maybe home is somewhere I'm going and never have been before."

Warsan Shire

Michael and Brianna's passage through their first portal to Wales was smooth, even though neither of them had done it before. They were guided by Mara, the highly skilled magician in Wales, who simply pulled them into the oak tree near the Marches and attracted them to her cottage in the Brecon Beacons. Brianna had learned about portals from her mother, even though she had never traveled through one. When she felt the pull, she knew immediately what was happening, and she trusted the magic. She wanted to keep her eyes open, to experience everything, but it was impossible. Her eyes closed as if she were falling asleep. Orangino nestled in his bag on Brianna's chest. This was nothing new to a magical cat. Brianna instinctively reached her hands out in the direction they were moving. Her intuition told her that it was important to focus on the destination, even though she didn't know what it was. Michael had simply fallen into the void, and he would have been frightened at the lack of control if he had time. He barely had time to take a breath when they landed in Mara's cabin. As soon as he saw Mara, who had sheltered him before sending him on his way to escort Brianna, Michael knew that whatever had just happened, they were both safe in Wales.

"Welcome. That was a narrow escape. A village witch hunt is nothing to make light of. I am Mara, Brianna. And I have been helping you along the way, along with your cat Orangino and your aunt Andera. I left a knife for you in the kitchen in Newark."

"You?! That was a girl! The one who told me she would be back to kill the cook!"

Mara's eyes twinkled with mischief. "Just one of my disguises. And I must say the kitchen maid isn't one of my favorites. And much as I would like you to stay and rest here, I have instructions to send you on your way. Brianna, your grandparents have some important things to tell you, and you need to be there, too, Michael."

"My grandparents?" Brianna asked.

"Who are her grandparents?" Michael asked.

Mara smiled. "It's not my place to answer your questions. I was simply instructed to send you on as fast as possible."

"Send us . . . . how?" Michael looked around the small cottage. He was just getting his bearings again after the dizzying ride through space from the Marches. "After that last journey . . ."

Mara's voice was light and crisp, like raindrops. "That was nothing. You are about to meet the most powerful magicians on this island. You are lucky they are in the same time period as we are. Time travel portals are even more prone to vertigo, and prone to error. But they will be ready for you, and attracting you from their end.

"Brianna, are you ready?" She turned to the young girl. "I want you to concentrate on your grandparents, your mother's parents, and hold Michael's hand. We will talk another time."

Brianna checked Orangino in his "nest," and was greeted with a contented purr. He reached out a paw and touched her chin, and she could have sworn he was smiling. She grasped Michael's warm hand, glad of his protection, even though she didn't need it now. She was where she was meant to be; she could feel it. Mara put a hand on each of their shoulders and gave a gentle push. Blackness. And then they stumbled into a large room, illuminated only by a roaring fire in the fireplace. Orangino leapt out and positioned himself in front of the fire, intent on a good grooming session. The first person Brianna spotted was her mother. She looked the same. Hair a bit disheveled, smudges of dirt on her skirt, and a smile on her face. How she had missed that smile! She ran to her. It had been so long.

"Brianna!!" Her mother Marged screamed. She ran toward her daughter, arms outstretched, but froze when she saw the man who accompanied her. "You." Her voice was flat, the joy and excitement gone.

Marged's mother stepped forward and lay her hand on her daughter's arm. "Marged. Be calm, please. You daughter needs to know the truth."

"No. She's <u>my</u> daughter. He left before she was born."

"He left? Or you left him?" said Rhys.

"Please," Brianna interrupted. "What are you talking about?"

Rhys looked at her husband, who nodded as he met her eyes. The older woman removed her hand from Marged's arm and stepped toward Brianna, at the same time Andera moved in place next to her sister, ready to handle any outburst that might erupt from the distraught woman.

"Brianna, my dear." She reached for the young girl's hands, which Brianna gave willingly into the firm grasp. "My name is Rhys. I am your grandmother, your mother's mother. The grouchy looking old man there is Jonathan, my husband, your grandfather. Some call him the most powerful wizard in England and beyond. That may be true, but I don't say it to his face for fear of building up his ego more than it is already." She turned and smiled at him, to which he raised his eyebrows in an expression of skepticism. "I hope your mother has told you something of us while you were growing up. I know she taught you some magic and gave you at least a grounding in our work."

Marged looked as if she wanted to add something, but Andera tightened her grip on her arm and she said nothing.

Rhys continued. "We are most happy to have you here. You have grown into a fine young woman, and we hope you may spend some time with us."

Marged grunted, but Rhys continued without so much as glancing at her daughter. "Every child has a mother and a father. Brianna, what has your mother told you of your father?"

"She told me that he abandoned us, that he left before I was born." Brianna looked at her grandmother with a clear, open countenance.

"That's not quite true, dear," her grandmother continued gently. "It is true that your father left before you were born, but it was very early in your mother's pregnancy. She wasn't even sure herself, and had said nothing to him of her suspicions. I know this to be true."

At this point Jonathan came forward and took one of Brianna's hands from the grasp of his wife. "My wife sometimes takes a long time to get to the point. Your father did not abandon you. Far from it. Your father has been guiding and protecting you for the past year, ever since you left the village. Brianna, Michael is your father."

Brianna turned to the tall man with the graying hair, the man she knew as Sir Michael. He was smiling in a strange, wistful kind of way. He opened his mouth to speak but then closed it again. Tears welled in Brianna's eyes as she thought of all the times he had been there for her since they met in Newark." You didn't know?"

"No," he said. "I swear I did not. I just knew I needed to take care of you, make sure you came to no harm. You showed up in a dangerous place and a dangerous time. I only learned the truth from Mara in Wales just before I left to meet you and accompany you across the Marches to the Brecon Beacons." He held out his hand to her, and she took it, allowing its warmth to envelop her small one.

Brianna sighed deeply and gazed around the room. These people were her family. Her magic family. Except for Michael. She didn't think he was magic, but maybe . . .

Brianna met Michael's gaze and her eyes blurred with tears. "I began to suspect something after I left Rowena and headed for Wales," he said softly. "She hinted at a secret involving the two of us. And I remembered Marged, and her magic abilities, which she was so desperate to forget when I knew her."

"No." Marged clenched and unclenched her fists in anger, although Andera still held her arm. "I don't want him in my daughter's life."

"Why not, Marged?" Her mother gazed at Marged intently.

"Because he's not magic. What would be his purpose in her life?"

"Oh, but he is magic," Her father stood in front of her, hands on her shoulders. "Look at me, Marged."

She raised her eyes tentatively. She had always been afraid of her father, but now she wondered why. There was such gentleness in his eyes. "Oh yes, he is magic," Jonathan continued. "But he never knew it, because he never knew his parents. The two of you created a most magical child, who is only just beginning to know her powers."

Marged was quiet then, and tears dripped from her eyes onto the stone floor. Finally she raised her head. "I would like to go back to the time in the future that I saw at Dover Castle. The young soldiers were so sad. I think I could help them."

"Not yet, dear Marged. Although I appreciate your generous thoughts. You need training, focus. You missed out on so much when you were young. It is not time for you to take on so grave a responsibility."

Marged bowed her head. *No use in arguing*, she thought. She would hold her thoughts to herself, but when she met his gaze, she knew that her father, the great magician, knew what was in her mind. He nodded his head abruptly. "Take care of her," he said to his wife. It was a command, and Marged did not like the sound of it. It had the sense of keeping her contained, rather than the caring she might have wished for.

"And you, Brianna," the great magician Jonathan stood and held out a long, bony hand to his granddaughter. "Have you found what you were searching for when you left the village with that orange cat?" Orangino, who had been grooming himself in the corner, meowed at the reference to his regal self.

Brianna did not know whether she should take the hand of the high magician, even though he was her grandfather, or curtsey as she would to a nobleman, but she was saved from making the decision when he wrapped his arms around her in a hug. "Welcome home, Brianna," he whispered into her hair. He released her, but continued to grasp her shoulders as he gazed into her eyes. She felt the magic course through her body and the power she had always known she possessed held her fast. She was home.

"Now, my dear," her grandmother Rhys spoke. "We will have much to speak of about your future. We have thought of sending you to Mara in Wales. She is one of the best magic teachers on the island, now that Rowena has passed to the next world." Brianna opened her mouth to answer, but her grandmother held up an elegant finger. "Time enough to discuss that later."

Brianna was surprised to see Orangino rub forcefully against her skirt. Back and forth with a firm head butt. Something brushed her leg, and she remembered. "I think I have something for you." She raised her head to her grandfather.

"Oh?" His piercing blue eyes bore into her, but there was humor there, too.

Brianna lifted the hem of her skirt and ripped the seam. She caught the jewels as they trickled into her hand. Orangino purred loudly as he sat watching. If he were an ordinary cat, the jewels would have made amusing playthings. But he was not an ordinary cat. Brianna stood and handed the jewels to her grandfather. "I believe these are yours."

"Thank you." The great magician took the jewels from her hand and raised his fist over his head. With a whoosh and a rainbow of colored stars, the jewels disappeared into the storeroom with the rest of the treasure.

"And this." Brianna handed her grandfather the remnants of the snow wren's nest. "I'm afraid it was crushed in the village where they were burning the witch."

"That's what was supposed to happened." He smiled as he took the delicate pieces from her. "That's how it protected you." He cradled the pieces in his cupped hands until they became a whole nest once again. With a twist of his wrist, the nest disappeared up the magician's voluminous sleeve. "There. It will be ready for whoever needs it next."

There was a small magical disturbance in the air, and Mara appeared. "Refreshments are here!" she called merrily. She snapped her fingers, and a long table covered in a snowy white tablecloth set itself across one end of the room. She snapped them again and the platters of succulent roast chickens with carrots, mushrooms and something called potatoes appeared. One end of the table groaned under the weight of an enormous cake decorated with walnuts and strawberries. The strawberries pulsed with ripe juiciness that caused the guests' mouths to water whenever they looked at it.

Rhys watched her husband, and she believed that she had never seen him smile so much, but both of them kept wary eyes on their daughter Marged, who in turn watched them. And she was quick. She eased herself toward the door leading to the outside corridor, where she knew there was a time/space portal, but continued her conversation with Brianna and Michael like they were one big happy family. All the time she kept focused on her mother, her father and her sister Andera. When she saw that the three of them were looking elsewhere, she smiled quickly at Michael and Brianna. "I'll be right back," she said, and was gone -- out the door, down the corridor, through the portal, and back to her soldiers who flew in the metal birds. Her family would leave her alone, she knew, at least for a while.

Brianna watched her go. "She won't be back. I know her, and maybe she will be better off. She needs to go her own way, but I will miss her."

Before Michael could answer, Andera interrupted. "She's gone, isn't she? I felt her go through the portal."

"Yes," Michael replied. "She went her own way, as she always has."

"I think mother and father knew that she would. They will ensure her safety from a distance, and keep her out of trouble, but they won't try to bring her back here again." Andera smiled. "She thought she was sneaking out, that no one would see her go, that if we did we would try to stop her. But it wasn't that way. We all knew she would go."

They were joined by Jonathan and Rhys. "We will keep an eye on her," Jonathan said. "But she needs to go her own way. I know both of you understand this."

Brianna looked at Michael, who nodded in agreement. "Yes," Brianna answered, "but what will I do now?"

Rhys smoothed Brianna's light brown hair off her cheek. "What would you like to do?"

"I think I need some time," she answered, gazing around the room where she knew so much magic happened. She could feel the strength of it. "Could I stay here for a while with both of you?" She looked to her grandfather, who smiled in a most unmagician-like way. "And Sir Michael -- I mean my father -- could he stay, too, so we can all get to know each other? After that I would like to learn more magic, and maybe then learn to understand my mother."

"I think that can be arranged," Rhys answered. "Mara has agreed to assist with further training, to continue what your mother awakened in you, and our dear Rowena continued."

She turned to Michael, who could have been her son-in-law. "And you, Michael? After you spend some time with your daughter, will you be ready to learn about the magic that was born in you, or do you wish to continue being a knight?"

Michael bowed his head in respect to the great witch. "I am done with working for a king. I seek a higher calling."

"We are grateful, Michael," Jonathan added. "You do realize that you will no longer use the title of knight."

"I do. I have no more need of that title, as I said."

"Excellent!" Jonathan clapped the younger man on the shoulder. "Let me show you to the room that will be yours whilel you are with us." The two men walked away, leaving the three women, Brianna, her aunt Andera, and her grandmother Rhys.

"Come." Rhys guided the other two out into the corridor through which Brianna's mother had disappeared just a short time before. "I want to show you something."

She stopped at an opening in the stonework, where they looked out at the stars shining down the medieval city of Lincoln, stars that shone unchanging over the centuries. "Those stars have been here since before this castle was built, since before Britons even walked in this land, and they will be there, twinkling in the night sky, until long after that war in the future that will be called a world war, the Second World War, to be precise.

"But people won't learn the futility of war, the pointlessness of greed, and that is why they lose their meaningless treasures. They think they can blame other people who lack the power that they enjoy, but they always lose in the end."

The three women stood in silence, contemplating the sky, the future of the land, themselves.

"Let's sleep," Rhys said at last. "We have much to do tomorrow." She kissed her daughter and her granddaughter and went back inside the main chamber.

Andera kissed Brianna and moved to the door, following her mother. "I'll see you in the morning," she whispered.

Brianna smiled and turned back to the stars, as an orange cat rubbed against her legs. "I'm finally home," she whispered into the night.

CPSIA information can be obtained
at www.ICGtesting.com
Printed in the USA
BVHW042233061218
535006BV00019B/259/P